Their Only Hope

BETTY ARRIGOTTI

Dedicated to lost children and lost childhoods. May the Good Shepherd carry the little ones gently in his arms.

iv

AUTHOR'S NOTE

Thank you to all my readers who have encouraged me to continue story telling. This tale is less "cozy" than others I've written, and I hope I won't disappoint your expectations. It is still a Christian love story; however, a little boy went missing from our community and his story is unresolved. I have purposely left the location of my story ambiguous, lest we think these things can't happen where we live.

With someone's child in danger, my heart could no longer look upon only what is noble, right, and pure. I needed to admit we stand in the darkness and yearn for the light. Yet, God is always there with us and faithfully draws us into his arms of love. He is our happy ending.

Prologue

Nine-year-old Ryan stepped off the bus downtown and scanned the sidewalk for his online friend. Jimmy had told him to wait near the bike shop if he was late, so Ryan sat down on the curb in front of the store. This suddenly didn't seem like such a good idea. It had sounded fun to explore downtown together for their first meeting in person, and Jimmy had even been nice enough to figure out which bus he would need. The plan was to spend an hour or so together and then Ryan could get back before his mom was home from work and she'd never know. He'd only been staying home by himself for a couple of weeks now. That had taken a ton of work to convince his mom he was old enough. But it hadn't turned out to be as fun as he thought it would be. Until he met Jimmy online. They really hit it off.

But, where was he? He studied the people near the bus stop and hoped he'd recognize Jimmy from his internet picture.

A big man sat down next to him. "Hi, are you Ryan?"

He nodded but wished he could say no.

"I'm Jimmy's dad. He hurt his ankle and couldn't make it

downtown, but I told him I'd come get you and bring you to our house. He'll be so glad to get to talk to you in real life, especially since he's sad about having to stay home with his sprained ankle. I bought him a new video game you two can play together. My car is right over there."

It was a cool car. Black, shiny, and with gold trim on the wheels, the handles, and even the leaping-cat hood ornament. But something about this didn't feel right. He'd give the man a test. "Did Jimmy tell you what game we play online?"

"Sure, Minecraft. He says you're really good at it, too."

OK, so he really must be Jimmy's dad. He relaxed a little. "I have to be home before 6:00."

"No problem. I'll even drive you so you don't need to take the bus."

Ryan followed the man to his car, wishing he was home playing on his computer. Wishing he had told his mom where he was going.

Knowing she never would have let him come.

Chapter 1

As she stepped onto the sidewalk, Virginia Shea tugged at her skirt. She'd prefer it were a foot longer, but what she wore wasn't up to her these days. She adjusted her blouse, too. It felt even tighter than usual. Not a good sign. Definitely not a good sign.

"Good mornin', Ginger!" The voice of her sweet old neighbor Bessie lightened her mood. She smiled up at the wizened face that looked down on her from a window above. Virginia loved those wrinkles. If she still owned a camera, she would have made a study of them. She used to take photos of old things; she appreciated subjects that had endured time. Olive trees. Tortoises. Sequoias. Mountains. She hadn't seen any of those for the last two years. Now she was limited to a few blocks of crowded, tired buildings, filled with dissatisfied, lonely people.

But she could still study old folks. Weathered faces like Bessie's whose lines lifted at the eyes, then deepened as they etched down her cheeks to the toothless grin.

"Good morning, Bessie! How are you this steaming day?" If only these buildings had air conditioning.

"Fair to middlin', darlin'. Not up to my usual hijinks. Could you do me a good turn?"

"Happy to." That was, assuming Shank or his stooges weren't watching and calculating how much money she wouldn't be making while she helped Bessie.

"You're a good girl. I don't listen to nobody who says different." The old lady lowered an envelope down in a basket on a rope for Virginia to reach. "Just the usual few groceries, if you don't mind."

Virginia glanced up and down the street. No sign of Shank or his informants. She waved at Bessie and hurried the three blocks to the market. After choosing the least expensive bread, peanut butter, applesauce, and two yams, Virginia made her way to the pharmacy aisle. She glanced around her and then dropped a pregnancy test into her basket, quickly covering it with the loaf of bread. She ignored the fear that clamored for her attention. She wouldn't worry, she told herself. Not yet. She'd taken all precautions. It had to be another false alarm. But a snag in her resolve forced a silent pleading, "Please, no. Please, no."

She paid for Bessie's groceries with the enveloped money and for her secret purchase with the last of her own. She slipped it into her purse beneath the condoms.

Virginia didn't make eye contact with the driver who slowed as he passed her on the way back to Bessie's. She'd need to make this delivery quick or Shank would be unhappy.

"God help me," she whispered. The words were hardly a prayer anymore. They had been at first, but help hadn't come. Now they were more a habit that kept her sane. They connected her to her Grandma Ruth, the one person who had loved her, and the one who long ago taught her to pray. The knowledge of what Virginia's life was like now would have killed the dear woman..., if she weren't already dead.

One of Shank's goons turned his car onto her street. She slowed to a seductive walk and stared him down as he drove by. As soon as he turned the corner she hurried to Bessie's.

No wrinkled face was watching out the window for her. Unusual and unfortunate. She had hoped for a quick delivery. "Bessie?" she called. No answer, so she ran up the stoop steps

4

and two flights inside the building to her door. Her knock brought no response. Come on, Bessie, she thought. Don't get me in trouble.

She couldn't leave the groceries outside the door. In this neighborhood, they wouldn't last long. She tried the door, thinking she could slip them inside. Of course, it was locked. She knocked again but, worried that the stooge would circle the block soon, she waited only a moment before she ran back down the stairs, outside, and up the fire escape. Bessie's window was open, and as Virginia stooped to reach the groceries through, she spotted Bessie lying on the floor.

"Please, God, no!" The refrain picked up where it had left off earlier. She climbed inside the window and ran to Bessie. The old woman roused enough to look at Virginia with terror in her eyes, the same fear she'd seen in a child's eyes only the night before. Virginia forced the memory out of her mind to focus on her friend, whose lovely wrinkles sagged down one side of her face.

Shank's gonna kill me, she thought. But what could she do? She wouldn't leave a friend helplessly lying on the floor. She called 911 from her cell phone, praying it would work. All the other features besides dialing the House had been disabled, even the camera. The call went through and she was glad for once that Shank insisted his girls carry them at all times. Pacing and wondering what Bessie would need, she gathered the dear woman's purse, keys, and the list of numbers she had seen next to the phone, then laid them alongside her friend. As sirens approached, she patted Bessie's hand reassuringly. "It's alright now, Bessie. They'll take good care of you." She unlocked the door but, having done all she could, scooted back out the fire escape window, closing but not locking it behind her. She needed to get to work.

From across the street, Virginia watched as paramedics carried Bessie down the stoop to the waiting ambulance. The goon drove past and she acknowledged him with a chin lift. When he was out of sight she raced up the fire escape and slipped into Bessie's apartment. She needed to take advantage of a private bathroom. A place to fumble through a pregnancy test.

Once back on the street, she waited the recommended number of minutes before opening her purse and peering in.

Earlier the same morning, Joseph O'Keefe resisted, knowing it was unnecessary, but then brushed his teeth for a third time, as usual. He scrubbed the sink with the bleach mixture he kept in a spray bottle for that purpose, rinsed it, and then donned his black seminary shirt and added the white clerical collar. One more check in the mirror, a meticulous hair combing, his daily request, "God, give me courage to follow your will," and he was ready to go.

With any luck—or God's providence—he corrected himself, the bishop would hire him by the end of today's interview. Then after next week's graduation and ordination, he could begin the path toward his own church and flock of believers. No more dormitory life sharing common rooms and common colds; no more cafeteria food, contaminated by coughs and lack of hygiene.

It was still dark but unusually warm for mid-May as he drove away from the seminary. In five hours, he should easily arrive in the city with ample time for lunch before his interview. Afterwards he'd need an overnight stay—he cringed at the thought of how much cleaning he would need to do in a room where countless people had stayed—but then he could reward himself with a bit of sightseeing before he started back to his town. His mind remained busy through the long drive with dreams of the future. Then, with less than ten miles to his destination, his hope for lunch went up in smoke, smoke that rose from the hood of his car.

Joseph signaled and exited the highway at the next ramp, then drove several blocks in a run-down neighborhood looking for a place to pull over and park. An ambulance flashed past him toward the highway and he bowed his head. "God, bless the people in need. Be with them in their time of trouble. Draw close and comfort them." He glanced up to see the smoke still rising from his engine compartment. "And thank you for providing an exit when my car needed it. Now please help me get to the interview on time."

He parked, climbed out of the car and raised the hood. Steam, not smoke, boiled out of the radiator. Not surprising, considering the heat that assailed him once he left his air-conditioned automobile. "Thank you, Father," he said. He would need only a few minutes for the car to cool before he could add enough water to get him to the interview and locate the trouble later.

Joseph looked around while he waited. This wasn't a part of town he'd have chosen to drive through, let alone stop in. The narrow streets were lined with run-down apartment buildings, and plywood covered the windows of many business fronts. Men in sleeveless T-shirts sat on the steps in front of some of the buildings. Inside, old ladies leaned out open windows to catch a breeze. He couldn't imagine living without air conditioning in this heat, but with so many windows open that must be the case for most everyone here.

Across the street, a young woman leaned against a light post and dried her eyes with quick finger swipes. Judging from the short skirt and tight top, he surmised she was a prostitute. He guarded his eyes and heart from her provocative stance. "God help her," he murmured. He couldn't imagine why a woman would ever lower herself to that business.

Go to her.

Joseph didn't receive prodding from God every day, but he recognized the thought wasn't his own. Yet it couldn't be from his Father. He prayed, "Lord, I'm headed to an interview to do your ministry. It's what we've been working toward for years now. Did I hear you right?"

Go to her.

The radiator would take a few more minutes to cool, anyway. He bowed his head in obedience. *All right, but lead me not into temptation.*

Starting across the street he could see, now that he allowed himself to look, how very pretty she was, or would be if it weren't for the suggestive clothes and heavy make-up. Her copper hair waved down past her shoulders. Her features were lovely and she seemed younger than his first glance had estimated. Maybe in her late teens. What a waste of a life.

When she noticed him, she wiped her eyes again with the back of her hand and stood taller, offering him a slow smile that didn't reach her eyes. "Hello, Rev'rend, you here to save me or to lose yourself?"

He had forgotten he was wearing his new clerical collar. *Oh, this must look very bad.* Thank heavens no one knew him around here. *Father, am I hearing you right?*

Silence.

"My radiator is cooling off and while I waited I noticed you crying. Are you OK?"

She responded with a smile that almost lit her eyes and a quick shrug. "Sorry. You never know."

He didn't like to think what her answer meant. Surely ministers weren't ever her... customers. He heard a car drive behind him and watched her gaze follow it. Her demeanor changed. She leaned her chest toward him and her mouth returned to the fake smile. Through the grin she whispered, "We're being watched. I have to make it look good."

He heard the car stop and a door slam. As Joseph turned, a surly looking, Sasquatch-sized man tapped his watch and said, "You're behind, Gin. Shank ain't happy." He met Joseph's eyes. "One of us is gonna raise a little hell with Ginger, Rev. Will it be you or me?"

If the words weren't enough, the terror in the girl's eyes told Joseph the threat was real. He slid his arm around her back, not quite touching, and guided her to his car. When he had settled her in the passenger seat, he poured his water bottle into the radiator. It would have to be enough for now.

As he hurried into the car he saw she'd buried her face in her hands. He could barely make out her words through her sobs. "I'm sorry. I'm so, so sorry."

Joseph forced his eyes away from her low-cut neckline and his mind from his involuntary thoughts. He raised his heart to God and added his own silent apology to hers. He hated that despite her distress and the threatening presence of the man, all he really wanted to do was wipe his hands with his antiseptic wipes. And his steering wheel. And, God help him, his sleeve in case he had touched her back to guide her to the car. He promised himself he would disinfect thoroughly once he was alone again.

"Let's get you out of here."

Blade watched the car hurry away, and quickly memorized the make, model, and license plate number. This was second nature to him. His job was to keep track of Shank's girls and he was good at it. Not that he was too worried about Gin. She'd accepted his training well and, other than taking off to the grocery store for the old lady now and then, she knew and followed the rules. Some girls took a little more convincing, but she was a quick study after the first time he cut her. Too bad, too. He took a certain pleasure in the occasional disciplinary action required when someone got mouthy or thought they could get away with not pulling their weight.

He remembered last night and grinned. Bunny had thought he wouldn't notice the extra $20 she kept back, but he knew it was tucked in her bra strap. Didn't stay there long. And his blade had left a not-so-gentle, but hidden reminder for her not to try that again. He caressed the knife in his pocket. Maybe Gin would slip up and he could do a little more disciplining. He knew she was behind in her count for the day, and he doubted any man in a minister's collar was going to make up the difference. They were always cheap. The thought gave him something to look forward to and take his mind off the heat.

With less than five minutes until his interview appointment, Joseph pulled into the church parking lot. The temperature struck him as soon as he turned off the engine and the air conditioner stopped. It must have topped 100 outside. He had intended to ask this Ginger person to wait in the car, but even with windows wide open it wouldn't be safe. He couldn't bring her in with him to the offices, of course. Not in that outfit. He hadn't looked at her again but he remembered it all too well. At least her crying had stopped.

"I need to get to an interview inside, but I can't leave you here or take you in with me."

She laughed a dull, single syllable. "No, I don't suppose so. We wouldn't quite make the impression you're hoping for, would we? I'll slip inside the church and say a prayer for my grandma. And one for you. Thanks for your help. I'll get myself back from here."

Her eyes widened.

"What's wrong?"

"I spent the last of my money on a... Never mind."

He pulled his wallet out. "Here, I'll give you—"

"No, you've done enough."

But at that instant Bishop Walters, his potential employer, walked up from behind the car to the driver's door. "Welcome, Joseph." He bent to look inside. "Oh, my."

Joseph looked to the bishop and back at the obvious prostitute in his passenger seat, then down at the wallet and money in his hands.

It was at that very instant that Joseph felt God's unmistakable urging. *Be her Hosea.*

Joseph followed the bishop into his office where two other ministers were waiting. Struggling to push what had just transpired away from his thoughts, he shook hands all around— more need for antiseptic later—and then sat, afraid that all his dreams for the future were lost. Still, he'd make the most of the interview and try to leave the rest in God's care.

The bishop took his chair at the head of the table, tented his fingers, and then grinned. "Before we begin with the formal interview questions, I can't wait to hear your explanation for the, uh, woman in your car."

The other two ministers turned toward Joseph, their surprise clearly evident both on their faces and in the way they sat forward in their chairs. This interview was certainly not going to be boring.

Joseph chose his words carefully, trying not to indict the young woman. Ginger's—if that was her name—career was her own story to tell, not his. He instead told them about his car trouble and that while waiting for it to cool, he had seen Ginger being threatened by a man and rather than leave her there, he had guided her into his car. He turned to the bishop. "When you arrived to welcome me at the car, I was about to give her bus money home."

Though all three men seemed a bit skeptical, if they didn't believe Joseph, they didn't say so.

Bishop Walters cleared his throat. "Shall we begin? Joseph, your work encouraging teens to be chaste and sexually abstinent has come to our attention. We've been told your workshops are well attended and well received."

"Thank you, Your Eminence. It's work I enjoy and hope to continue on a larger scale." He was relieved to be talking about anything other than the woman in his car, and on this particular subject he felt very capable. God had blessed his seminarian internship and brought him recognition among the leaders of the regional church. He breathed a prayer of thanks.

"We've been considering expanding our young adult program," the bishop continued, "and are looking for the right person to lead it. You are among the candidates."

Something in the bishop's voice led Joseph to hear, *At least you were until I found a prostitute in your car.* But he placed that worry in God's hands. Or he tried. The position the bishop was describing was a rare opportunity and one that Joseph dearly wanted. It was what had caused him to drive 200 miles to this city in hope of securing the job. Just days from seminary graduation, deacon ordination, and his Master of Divinity Degree, he was ready to take the next steps on God's path. A path that he expected would culminate in leading a parish someday— his own flock of believers to encourage.

Joseph answered the questions he was asked and felt, with God's help, he represented himself quite well. Soon this uncomfortable day of unexpected turns would be over. With a little providence, he'd be back to school with a job offer in hand to show his mother when she came to the graduation ceremonies.

Surely, he had misunderstood, or maybe imagined, the Hosea prompting.

Virginia watched the young man follow the bishop, and the erect way he carried himself made her suspect he'd been a soldier. They disappeared into an office building next to the church. She hadn't been in a place of worship for more than two years, but this day wasn't like any other day in all that time. She had told the reverend she'd go in the church and say a prayer for her grandma. That was more information than she usually shared with anyone. She'd have to be more careful. But the afternoon was hot and the car was already an oven, so she walked to the door and slipped inside. With relief, she observed the dark church was empty. The air felt almost cold in comparison to outside, and she shivered a little.

Virginia sat in the back row and looked at the altar in front. She'd intended to pray, but what good had that done her? When she last attended another church like this, she'd sat with her grandma at her side, enveloped in the sense of security her presence always provided. That was back when she believed God would be her help whenever she needed him, back when life was secure and she was loved.

She missed her grandma desperately still. If only she could talk to her again. Well, why not? If there was a heaven, Grandma Ruth surely would be there, and maybe she could hear her.

Bowing her head, she whispered, *I miss you every day. I'm so sorry for what I've become. I didn't mean for it to happen. When you died, they took me to a foster home. The parents were fine, but their son Jake...* She couldn't allow herself to think about him and what he'd done to her. Those thoughts had broken her before, and she needed to stay strong to survive.

I ran away, Grandma. I had to. But I ran from bad to worse. Now I can't get out of it. And when Shank finds out I'm pregnant, he'll make me have an abortion. Even if I survive not making any money for him today, this little baby will die. She felt tears running down her face but she didn't bother to wipe them away. No one could see her here.

Grandma, maybe you can talk to God. He doesn't hear me, and I guess I don't deserve him to, but could you ask him to help my baby? She's so innocent and vulnerable.

When the interview ended, Joseph walked to his car and, to his relief—immediately followed by guilt—found it empty. Then he remembered the bishop's arrival at the car had kept him from giving Ginger any money. If she really was broke, she wouldn't be too far away. He walked to the church, realizing both that its dark coolness made it the most likely place for her to be and that his disrupted spirit could use a little time with the Source of Peace.

When the door groaned shut behind him, he used the dark to squirt his palms with sanitizer and rub vigorously, grumbling a bit to himself at the thought of all the hands he'd shaken, not to mention the church door latch that countless others had touched.

It took a few moments before his eyes adapted to the low light, but there she sat in the last row, her back straight but her head bowed. He knelt across the aisle from her. After he had prayed for a few minutes—prayed for guidance and understanding and *please, please let me be mistaken about what you want*—he stood and went to her. She turned, and for a moment he glimpsed softness, but then her fake smile returned and hardened her features.

He could have taken her back to her neighborhood, maybe even given her all the cash in his wallet to stave off the thug, if not for the black smudges below her eyes. Though not a trace of moisture remained, the girl obviously had been weeping. Every self-protective fiber in him said to run, yet he asked, "Can I buy you an early dinner?"

She shrugged with one shoulder, as if too tired to raise the other.

Ten minutes later Virginia excused herself while Joseph selected a booth in a coffee shop. Once in the bathroom, she looked in the mirror and would have sworn if she hadn't promised herself never to start talking like the other girls. She hated anyone to see her cry, but her smeared mascara announced her weakness to the world. She scrubbed it all away, every bit of makeup. Pulling a comb and an elastic band from her purse, she captured her mane into a polite pony tail. She could do that much for the minister, though she couldn't do anything about her clothes.

When she returned and sat across from him in the booth, she noticed his posture again as he stared intently at the menu.

She read hers only long enough to find the cheapest meal, then she broke the silence. "I'm Ginger."

He looked up at her.

"I mean Virginia. I go by Ginger, or Gin, for my work." She felt the blood rush to her cheeks and broke eye contact. She whispered once more, "Sorry."

While pretending to read the menu, she processed the change she had noted in his face when he glanced up and had seen her without makeup. She had to admit she felt a bit undone by his look. Like he could see the girl she used to be.

She sensed rather than saw him lean forward. "I'm Joseph. Joseph O'Keefe. Shall we start fresh?"

While thinking, *If only I could,* she offered her hand. He seemed reluctant to take it and the hesitation made her feel dirty. When he did take her hand, she gave it one shake, and answered his offer of a fresh start with a nod. "I hope the interview went well." *And that I didn't ruin it for you.*

"Hard to say." As he told her about the position he was applying for, she could hear in his voice how very much he wanted it. From what he said about his experience, he'd be perfect for it. But when he began to talk about his abstinence workshops, his words stumbled.

"I'm sorry," he said. "I didn't mean to sound judgmental."

She shrugged. "I'd be the first to tell the teens you're right. I wouldn't recommend—" she lowered her voice for the next two words— "casual sex to anyone."

He looked surprised and though he had said he didn't mean to sound judgmental, she could read accusation in his eyes.

For a moment, she wanted to explain how this had all happened. About the rape, the running away, the fateful trust she placed in Shank when he first comforted her. She reminded herself she couldn't trust any man, even one who seemed as nice as Joseph. She sighed. "This wasn't my choice."

Joseph couldn't believe the difference in the young woman who came out of the bathroom and sat across from him. She looked wholesome and, in spite of the guardedness of her eyes, quite striking. He had made a habit of thanking God as he

14

encountered beauty in the world and he did so now. *Praise, Father, for making such a lovely person. Guard my mind as I talk to her.*

He wasn't able to get much out of her about herself, but when she said prostitution wasn't her choice, he asked, "Why do you stay? Can't you leave?"

"Shank, my... boss, has eyes everywhere. His thugs make sure we don't stray far. We can get in a guy's car, but someone will have memorized the license plate, and if we aren't back in an hour or so they'll find us. Men never take us far anyway, but Shank always seems to know where we are. He texts us if we haven't checked in soon enough."

Joseph checked his watch. They'd been gone almost three hours. "He hasn't contacted you?"

As if her life depended on it, she snatched up her purse and dug through it. "My phone isn't here!" Her eyes were wide with fear. "I must have left it somewhere. Maybe at Bessie's. I was a bit frantic there."

"You'll be in trouble."

"Nothing I haven't handled before." She laughed, but he could read the distress in her eyes.

Now a good half-hour drive from where he had picked her up, and without the tracer app he assumed was on her cellphone, he realized no one was likely to find her. He was her chance, maybe her only chance to get away. Was this what God meant by being her Hosea?

His mind went back to the Old Testament story he read that morning. God told Hosea, his prophet, to find a prostitute and marry her as a symbol of how Israel had become like an unfaithful wife to him by adoring false gods. Hosea obeyed and married Gomer. Joseph always felt sorry for Hosea. It didn't seem fair to have to take a fallen woman as his wife, just to make a point to the Hebrews. He had to admire Hosea's obedience though.

Joseph had been afraid that, like Hosea, God wanted him to marry this Ginger. Now with relief he laughed at himself. At his deacon ordination, he intended to promise God to spend his life as a single man. Celibacy was a gift of self he wanted to present to the Father. Surely God honored that plan and was only asking Joseph to help Ginger break away from her oppression.

His worry lifted like a helium balloon. "Ginger,"—did her eyes darken when he used that name? —"surely you have family I could help you get to. I'd be happy to send you safely to them."

She blinked several times and he had the distinct impression she commanded her eyes to stay dry. "Please call me Virginia. You're not one of my customers. But no, there's no one."

His relief balloon popped. "No one? No siblings or cousins or friends or ..."

She was shaking her head slowly. "No one. Grandma Ruth died and she was my only family."

"But I can't let you go back!" He heard the rise in his voice that belied the calm he wanted to portray.

"I'll be fine."

He knew it was a lie.

She seemed to want to reassure him. "I prayed in that church, you know."

Despite an increasing fear of God's will, he asked, "Did you receive any answer?"

"Well, God and I aren't exactly on speaking terms, if that's what you mean. I asked Grandma to help me. If anyone goes to heaven, I'm sure she's there. She'll ask God for me."

"I'm sure she will, but why didn't you ask him yourself?"

"I gave up on that a long time ago."

Joseph's conscience burned. He sat across from a lost lamb who needed to find God again, and he was trying to get rid of her as quickly as possible.

Virginia's cynical chuckle made him think she'd read his mind.

"I did have a strange experience, though," she said. "I couldn't get Grandma's old Gomer Pyle reruns out of my head." She shook her head. "Not exactly church-appropriate thoughts."

His heart gave a jump. Gomer. Hosea's wife, Gomer. Like it or not, this *Virginia* seemed to be his Gomer. *Please God, let this mean you want me to rescue her from prostitution, not that you expect me to marry her.*

16

She was certainly beautiful enough to make someone want to marry her, though she was very young and her clean face gave her an innocent attractiveness. While she talked, he studied her wavy auburn hair, and creamy skin. Golden flecks highlighted her green eyes. He could clearly see a sprinkle of freckles across her little nose. He allowed his glance to sweep down to her curvy lips and then commanded it back to her eyes. Against his will, he remembered her too-tight blouse, but he would not look.

He was afraid the slight heat he could feel creep up his neck would announce his thoughts. Just the possibility made his pulse increase. Or was it her smile?

He forced his thoughts to prayer. The practice had served him well in the past. But turning his mind to God brought back his fear of becoming Hosea. His heartbeat quickened.

Just then the waitress came to take their order. She carried their two glasses of water by the rims and the thought of the contamination she smeared where his lips would touch overpowered any other worries.

The dinner passed in small talk and awkward silences.

When the waitress brought back his credit card, Virginia said, "I need to get back."

Her words broke Joseph's reverie and raised his anxiety. He couldn't imagine taking her back to the world where he found her. He didn't want to think about what that Shank guy might do to her.

"You can't go back." But God help him, every fiber in his body wished she could. He imagined dropping her off, then scouring the car with his antiseptic wipes.

"I have to." She paused and then the dread on her face lifted. "But if you aren't in a hurry, could you take me somewhere else first? After that I can get myself back if I can have bus money."

"Of course, I'm not driving home until tomorrow and I planned to get a hotel until then. Where do you want to go?"

"A friend of mine went to the hospital today and I'd love to visit her. I can't get into much more trouble than I'm already in anyway." She lifted her shoulders like his teenage sister Meg often did to indicate she didn't care one way or another, when she obviously cared a lot.

The hospital. Of all the places he hated, hospitals topped the list. Remembered smells and gore made him inhale sharply. Scenes flooded in from a lifetime ago, before seminary, when he had been a medic with the Army. A time before his fears had shifted, back when the enemy carried rifles in a desert, rather than lurking in unseen bacteria.

But he couldn't return her to her neighborhood, so this request would give him time to figure out what to do with her instead. He nodded, rose from the table and followed her back to his car. From behind, he watched her ponytail bounce like it belonged to a girl without a care in the world, but he knew her face belied the effect.

Virginia directed Joseph to the hospital and he found a space to park on the first level of its garage.

She turned to him with a cheery bravery. "Will you come in with me?"

Lord above, she had no idea what she was asking of him. "I can't," was all he could say. "But I'll wait."

"You don't need to. If you give me a couple dollars I can catch a bus from here."

"My mother taught me to always see a girl safely home. I'll wait and we'll figure out what to do when you're back."

She lifted her shoulders again in that don't-care-but-really-do way and hurried from the car. She struck him to be more like his sister than he'd realized. Not in clothes or demeanor, of course. His sister was a modest girl, but Ginger's—Virginia's—vulnerability made him want to protect her every bit as much as he would his Meg.

"Right," he told himself, "some guardian you are. You can't even accompany her into a hospital." But she had asked the impossible. The mere thought of the illnesses, diseases, and bacteria brought back the shakes he had fought so hard to overcome after his tour of duty as a medic.

He prayed. He knew it would help calm him eventually.

Chapter 2

Ginger hadn't been seen for three hours!?! Blade pulled out his phone and checked his tracking app. The girls didn't know that was one of the reasons Shank had given them phones. Stupid bimbo! She'd gone too far. *Nobody disappears for three hours and gets away with it.* None of the guys had been able to find the car she left in. They should have reported her to him long before this. They were all worthless.

Good. She wasn't far, in fact right next door to The House. He pounded on the apartment door of the old toothless lady. Gin should know better than to spend so much time off the street. He grinned. He'd have good reason to give her some *reminders* tonight. His hand stroked the knife in his pocket tenderly.

No answer.

"Gin, I know you're in there. Open the door!"

He didn't wait long before he kicked the door open, and he swore when he found the place empty. Checking his phone again, he located Gin's cell in the bathroom.

Well, it was her own fault that he'd tell the boss. *Shank*

will have lots to talk to you about tonight, Gin, he thought. *And then he'll turn you over to me for a little re-education.* By their unspoken agreement, Shank would let him be the one to set the girl straight when she got back. He licked his lips and squeezed the switchblade.

He left the apartment without taking anything. There wasn't much to offer anyway, but he made a point of not lining his pockets too close to home. He walked to the building next door and took a quick inventory of which girls were where. No sign of Ginger and no one had seen her for the last few hours. He knocked on Shank's door.

"Yeah?"

He let himself in. "Hey, Shank. Ginger's missing." He studied the room, not wanting to look directly at Shank for too long. Even after all these years, he still could be unnerved, and he wasn't sure why.

"How long?"

"Three hours now. I just found out. We've got the plate number but no sign of the car."

"And her phone?"

Blade was irritated that Shank might think he hadn't considered that but didn't let it show. "She left it in the old lady's place next door. No one's there."

"An ambulance took somebody out of the building a while ago. Heard it was the old lady. Maybe she went with her."

"I'll check the hospital."

"No, leave that to me. I'll send her to you when I find her. You can… remind her of the rules." The last he said with a cold smile, but it put Blade at ease. He wasn't in trouble, then. But Ginger sure would be. Blade hesitated, but then turned to go.

"Blade?"

He turned to face Shank again. "Yeah?"

"Something else is bothering you," Shank said with neither warmth nor malice.

Did he dare ask? Blade shrugged. "What's up with the little boys?"

"You trust me, don't you, Blade?"

"I do. I always have. We're always there for each other."

"Ever since we were kids." Shank locked his gaze on Blade.

Blade remembered the night they had begun to rely only on each other. The first time he'd used his knife to protect Shank and the first time Shank had used his smarts to protect Blade. Shank had taken the bloody knife, wiped off the hilt, and laid it in his mother's open hand. She was passed out from drinking. Her boyfriend was dead next to her. Now no one would suspect the boys he terrorized. The sons she didn't love enough to protect.

"You're the brains. Always have been."

"Then trust me on this. The boys are a lesson to their parents. They should take better care of them. And when they don't, then they must pay to get them back. We get the payoff; the parents get the boys. Lesson learned."

Blade relaxed. He'd been afraid the boys were for something else. Something he'd lived through and didn't want to put any other boys through. He should have known better than to doubt Shank.

Shank rose and drew his cashmere coat closer around his thin body. "Now, I'll go get Ginger, who also needs a lesson learned."

Virginia approached the hospital information desk. "Could you tell me what room Bessie Alvarez is in?"

"Are you family?" The receptionist began typing the name into the computer.

Worried they wouldn't let her see her dear friend, Virginia considered lying, but stuck to her code of ethics, such as it was nowadays. "No, I called 911 when I found her unconscious and I heard the medics say they were bringing her here." She smiled like there wasn't a reason in the world to keep her from seeing her friend.

The receptionist studied her and, once again, Virginia wished her blouse weren't tight and her skirt short. She remembered she had washed away the layers of makeup and hoped the ponytail would contradict her clothes.

Just when she had given up hope, the receptionist looked both ways, whispered, "Room 619," and pointed her toward the elevators.

When she found the room, Virginia tapped lightly on the door and pushed it open. In the first bed, a woman glanced her way for only a moment before returning her attention to a television. Virginia walked beyond the curtain room divider and grinned to see Bessie awake, though she looked tiny and frail.

The wrinkles Virginia loved lifted in recognition but only on one side of Bessie's face. "Ginger, my girl!" Her words sounded a bit more slurred than her usual toothless speech. "So good to see you! Now tell me how one minute I was home, and the next thing I knew I woke up here."

"When I got back with your groceries you wouldn't answer the door so I climbed up the fire escape and found you passed out. I dialed 911 and then skedaddled. I had to get back. I'm sorry I couldn't stay."

"No apologies needed, my dear. Sounds like you saved my life." She reached out and squeezed Virginia's hand, then held on like a child needing security. "Slight stroke, they say. They've notified my Jackson."

"That's wonderful! Well, not the stroke part. But you've been missing your son and now he'll surely come see you, won't he?" She knew he wasn't a bad son, just too busy.

"He called and said he's on his way. He wants me to move in with him and his missus."

The joy on Bessie's face made Virginia feel better than she had all day. She gently hugged the old woman. "I'm happy for you, but I'll miss you."

Bessie turned serious. "Ginger, girl, if I could take you away from the neighborhood with me, I would in a heartbeat."

The words reminded her of the strange young reverend who waited for her in his car. Good hearted, but naive. He wanted to fix everything, too, but she was in too deep. He didn't know about the baby. Shank didn't either, but that wouldn't last long. At the thought of her boss, she realized Joseph and Bessie were both right. She needed to get off the streets. She'd tried and failed before, but now it had become a matter of her little one's life or death.

Virginia squeezed Bessie's hand. "I'm getting out.

Whatever it takes."

"God help you, Girl." The old woman had tears in her eyes, and Virginia realized she did as well.

After one last hug, she left her friend behind, assured she'd be released into good hands. But as Virginia stepped out of the elevator, she heard a voice that stopped her in her tracks and made her wish the doors hadn't already closed behind her. Shank himself was talking to the receptionist. She tiptoed across the hall into a nearby restroom, heart racing as she prayed he hadn't seen her. With the door eased open enough to peek out, she could hear the receptionist say, "Popular lady, your mother. You're the second person to ask about her in just a few minutes. Room 619."

Virginia closed the door and held her breath until she heard the elevator open. She risked peeking enough to see Shank's back as he entered it, then she closed her door again before he turned to select the floor. No one else wore a long cashmere coat in the summer. If he traced her cell phone to Bessie's house, he must have guessed his missing girl might visit the old woman. Paralyzed from fear until she heard the elevator doors close, she needed a few moments to find her courage. After a peek from the restroom door assured her he was gone, she hurried past the receptionist and, once outside, ran to where Joseph had parked.

Please, God, let him be there!

Joseph had finished sanitizing the car interior with barely enough time for the moisture to evaporate when he glanced up and saw Ginger running toward him. One look at the fear in her face raised all his anxieties to full alert.

She jumped into the car and yelled, "Go, go! Get out of here fast!"

He prayed the radiator would stay cool long enough for them to get far from whatever or whomever had frightened this young woman so badly. Before he knew more, they found the highway and sped out of the city and in the direction of his home. When his heart had slowed a bit, he forced himself to make the car do the same. No sense drawing attention by going over the speed limit.

After a few more moments, Virginia seemed to calm herself as well.

He glanced at her and asked, "Want to tell me what happened?"

She described her narrow escape, and Joseph found himself watching cars in his rearview mirror, wondering if any tailed him. An hour into their drive a sign advertised a shopping mall, and he decided to exit the highway. Keeping an eye out for any cars that might follow, he drove to the mall and parked.

He removed his clerical collar and then turned to her. "Virginia, I don't want to insult you but would you mind terribly if we bought you a different outfit? And you'll need a few overnight supplies. I'm not taking you back there."

"I'm sorry to be more trouble and expense." Her eyes still held tears. "But there's nothing I'd like better than to never wear these clothes again."

Virginia bypassed the larger department stores and stopped in a discount shop. With Joseph's encouragement, she picked out an inexpensive pair of black pants, a skirt, a sweater, and a couple shirts. He was relieved that she chose modest clothes, but he waited awkwardly while she bought underwear and a pair of pajamas. Once all the items were paid for, Virginia changed into one of the new outfits and left her old life's clothes behind.

Joseph suggested a variety store for personal supplies.

"I have most of what I need in my purse. We had to be ready to freshen up between…"

As her voice trailed off, one look at her blushing defenselessness assured Joseph he had done the right thing. Still, he asked himself again how this had all happened so fast and what lay ahead.

For instance, where would they spend the night? He couldn't risk that someone might recognize him checking into a hotel with a woman. But the emotional toll of the day left him too exhausted to drive much farther.

Back in the car, Virginia considered Joseph as he drove. He wasn't a bad looking young man. Dark short hair, kind brown eyes, a gentle manner. But she'd thought Shank was kind and gentle when she'd first met him, two years ago. That was all an act to get her to trust him, and then when she did, when she let herself care for him, he used her himself before he charged others to use her, too. She had to be careful not to let herself be duped ever again. Every man she'd met in the last two years, and there'd been more than she could count, cared only about himself. Not her. Not the wives their rings attested to.

She checked Joseph's left hand. "You're not married," she said matter-of-factly.

He laughed. "Not even close."

"No girlfriend?" He might be interested in men. That would explain him not hitting on her. "Guy friend?"

He looked at her with wide eyes and his neck colored a bit. She liked that about him. He didn't seem able to hide his emotions.

"I'm pretty much a loner."

"Unusual for a reverend, isn't that? I picture them being real people persons." She regretted the words when she saw his face cloud.

"I'm not quite a reverend yet. I graduate next weekend and will be ordained as a deacon then."

"But the collar?"

"That was dressing officially for the job interview."

"You seem older than a college graduate."

Joseph glanced over at Virginia momentarily, then returned his attention to the highway. "I started to study pre-med after high school. Two years in, my dad died, shot while on duty. I'm not at all like him. He was a real man's man, if you know what I mean. He started out in the military, then moved into police work. But when he died I wanted to honor him, so I enlisted in the Army. Did a tour overseas in the Middle East, where I was a medic. But I met a chaplain there that set me on a new direction with my life."

She congratulated herself on pegging him as a soldier earlier. "He must have been quite a man."

"Woman, actually. She was a Quaker minister. All the soldiers loved her. Most of them because she was pretty, but I loved her spirit and wanted the faith she had."

"She was with your troop in a combat zone?" Virginia didn't understand why, but this woman was making her feel very inadequate by comparison. A woman going off to war for her country and her God. What had Virginia done by comparison?

"No, she was the chaplain at an Army hospital. She helped me recover after I was wounded."

Virginia suddenly felt small for her self-centered thoughts. "Wounded?"

"Took a bullet to the shoulder. I'm OK now, but it sent me stateside for physical therapy after a shoulder replacement." Joseph's face did more than cloud. It shut down entirely in a look Virginia had seen on other men's faces. It meant don't go there. No more questions.

She sighed. "I'm glad you're all better."

All better. That's what the world saw when they looked at him. He had returned from combat wounded and now looked all better. Fixed. Healed. Recovered.

But that's not the whole story, Joseph thought. Yes, his shoulder was almost as good as new, apart from reduced range of motion. However, his soul wasn't. Or his mind. He longed to find the person he used to be back when germs didn't occupy way too much of his time and his thoughts. It wasn't simply his wound that had changed him, but the wounds of countless others. Blood he had sopped up, bones he had seen shattered, intestines no longer contained where they belonged. The smell of gangrene and infection, and always the chance of contracting blood borne diseases. Their training to prevent the contraction of hepatitis and AIDS had terrified him.

He felt the shiver run through his body, the tremor that always began the uncontrollable shaking. He looked down at his hands, the place most likely for others to notice his trembling. He gripped the steering wheel tighter while taking deep breaths to forestall the reaction to his memories. And he prayed.

His mind grasped at memorized prayer, bits and pieces that were like lifelines when his mind approached panic. *Angel of God, my guardian dear...* That one was back from his earliest memories. He cast around for another more appropriate mantra. *Our Father, who art in heaven.* Yes, that was Jesus' prayer. It always helped. *Hallowed by thy name...* He made it as far as *deliver us from evil* before he began to feel the calm warm him. He reached out again for memorized Bible verses. *For God has not given us a spirit of fear and timidity, but of power, love, and self-discipline.* He had found solace in the book of Timothy before. It was one of his favorites. Another from Matthew, *For out of the heart come evil thoughts—murder, adultery, sexual immorality, theft, false testimony, slander. These are what defile a person; but eating with unwashed hands does not defile them."*

If only he could convince his wounded mind that unwashed hands would do him no harm. But as for sexual immorality, he had taken that warning fully into his soul. He came alive whenever he talked to teens about abstinence and purity. And yet, here he was seated a foot away from a woman, a girl—for surely now without the makeup she seemed more a girl than a woman—a girl who personified sexual immorality.

He glanced at her again, now dressed modestly and looking very much like she could be one of his sister's classmates. She certainly didn't seem defiled.

At that moment, she turned to him with concern in her eyes and smiled encouragement. The smile slowed his heart from its sprint. Her face did as much to warm and calm him as his prayers usually did.

But as suddenly as her smile had begun, it changed and hardened. She turned away and gazed out at the road, crossing her arms.

Get hold of yourself, Virginia Marie! She wouldn't let it happen again. She couldn't allow a man into her trust. It was high time she started relying on herself. She needed to make a new start, and yes, this guy had gotten her off the streets for the moment, but she needed a plan for her baby's sake, a job and a place to live. She was determined to seize this opportunity and make a new future for herself. One that didn't include men. But how?

She didn't have a high school diploma. She had never

learned to drive. She had no work experience she could own up to. And as of tomorrow, she'd be 18 and no longer eligible for foster care. Not that she'd want to go down that road again. So, the plan became more immediate. Where would she sleep tonight? What would she eat tomorrow? She was homeless again, just like after she ran away at 16, and homeless girls are easy prey when they get hungry enough.

Outside the car window, the miles passed steadily. He was taking her away from all she knew, and that was good, but it also meant she wouldn't have anyone else to assist her. She watched the white stripes be swallowed one after another as the car passed them. In her rearview mirror, they accumulated behind her. So far from a danger she knew, but drawing ever closer to the unknown.

A sigh escaped her. She hated it, but she needed this man's help. Still, she was wiser than last time she ended up alone on the streets. She'd make sure he wouldn't make it into her heart. Make sure he couldn't take advantage of how easily she could love people.

Joseph was racking his mind, trying to figure out what to do with Virginia. He was afraid if he stayed on the road much longer, his emotional drain would make him unsafe to drive. At the next town, he exited. He parked in a well-lit lot near a convenience store.

"Where are we?" Virginia asked.

He pulled out his wallet and then looked at Virginia, seeing fear clearly fill her eyes. Quickly he handed her a $20. "Would you go in and buy us some sandwiches? I'm starved again and I need to figure out what to do next. I'm going to check my phone for ideas."

She took the money and entered the store but kept looking back at the car.

She's afraid I'll leave her, he realized. The thought surprised him with the strength of its temptation. Instead, he pulled out his phone and searched for a YWCA. He couldn't risk someone seeing him go into a hotel with a woman. He could pay for her to spend the night at the Y, and go to a hotel himself. No temptation, no scandal. Unfortunately, also no YWCA, either. The closest one was not far from his seminary, and he really couldn't drive that distance tonight.

Virginia returned with three hotdogs, handing Joseph two. She had also bought two bottled waters and two apples.

"Thanks," he mumbled and tried not to think about how her hand had touched the bun. Then he tried not to think of how many other hands had touched the bun. Or the apples. He couldn't help it. Or hide it any longer. He opened the glove box in front of Virginia and took out his antiseptic wipes. While she watched in silence, he polished the apple with one, then ran another one quickly over the hot dog buns. Sheepishly, he offered her the container.

Virginia smoothed the surprise off her face and accepted one, then polished her apple. She opened the plastic bag the water and apples had been in and tossed the towel into it, then held it open for Joseph to do the same.

"I have a problem with germs," he said.

She looked at him until he met her eyes, then said, "Thanks for waiting for me."

While they ate, Joseph told her of his dilemma about lodgings.

He seemed overly cautious to her, but she said, "I can sleep in the car." It was better than some places she had slept.

"No. Two separate hotels?"

She shrugged.

He let out a deep breath. "I'm being dogmatic. We aren't going to do anything wrong. We'll get two rooms tonight, non-adjoining, of course."

He noticed the relief in Virginia's face and realized his worries ran small compared to hers. Still, her concerns had become his now. Where would she spend the nights ahead?

After a weak attempt at sanitizing the room, Joseph fell asleep as soon as he settled into bed...

So very thirsty. He felt his throat had been parched longer than he'd been alive. His skin burned and, now completely dehydrated, he'd moved beyond perspiring. His only thought was for water and he could hear rushing, quenching water higher up beyond his path. He just needed to keep climbing towards the sound. He couldn't even swallow to soothe his throat. He put one foot in front of the other, struggling toward the enticing noise. He turned a curve in the path and he could see it! A waterfall cascaded down the mountain, gurgling and flowing toward him. Such joy! He'd be saved! He knew he wouldn't have lasted much longer but now he could reach the waterfall and live!

But then he came to a deep chasm too wide to cross! It was torture to see and hear the life-giving water and yet be stopped by a gap he couldn't breach. He looked desperately to his right and left but there was no way across. He realized with terror that his feet were sliding down the path and unstopped, he would plunge to his death. He flailed his arms to save himself and grabbed hold of a tree trunk. Even the tree was barely enough to keep him from falling, but as he wrapped his arms around it, he found handcuffs chained to it. He fastened one around his wrist, with only seconds left to spare before he would have slipped down the eroding edge. He could look over it now and the sight paralyzed him. The ledge plunged steeply down and below flowed molten lava.

He clung to the tree, testing the chain. It was secure. He was safe. But he was dying of thirst! The sight of the lava below was so mesmerizing he could not look away. "God, help me!" he screamed, though he could not hear his own voice over the bubbling flow of the burning liquid below. His gaze could not be torn from his feet at the edge and the lava below. Then he felt something moving against his feet - a small green tendril pushed at his toes. He wondered how it could be alive in such arid conditions. But not only was it alive, it was visibly growing!

What had been a tendril soon became a sturdy vine. He dared to focus his attention on it, rather than the precipice, and more tendrils emerged from the vine and spread along it, curving and weaving until the vine had become a bridge of sorts that stretched across the abyss. If only he had the courage to test it and see if it would support his weight, for it seemed the only possible means of escape. He forced his gaze away from the depths below him and raised his eyes toward the heights where he knew the waterfall to be. There, across from him, a giant of a man clung with one hand to the vine. With his other arm he reached toward Joseph, extending an offer of help.

Joseph looked back down and his courage escaped him. He was safe right now with the chained handcuffs holding him back from the slippery edge. Yet, he would need to remove them to reach out his arm and accept the offered help. If he did, wouldn't he surely fall? Would the man be strong enough to pull him across the chasm? He was safe for the time being, but so very thirsty!

"Grab hold! I can help you across!"

He realized the man had been calling out to him all this time but he hadn't been able to hear him.

"Fear is an illusion!" His rescuer called. "It's your fear holding you back!"

Again, Joseph looked at the chain. He might die if he reached out to the man, but he would surely die of thirst if he didn't. He took a terrified breath, released himself, and reached out while sliding toward the edge and the man. They clasped hands and he was drawn across the chasm.

He embraced his savior. "Thank you! Thank you!" he cried.

Broad leaves of the vine had caught the overspray of the waterfall and the man motioned for Joseph to drink from them. When his thirst had been sweetly quenched, Joseph turned to the burly man, who pointed back toward the chasm. Joseph could see another poor soul grabbing the chain to secure herself before she might fall. He recognized the terror in the woman's face as what he had felt only moments before. His rescuer had disappeared, so he grasped the hefty vine, wrapped one arm into it, and stretched toward her. "Grab hold! I can help you across!"

She didn't seem to hear him, her attention was so taken by the dire situation she was in. Then Joseph watched the vine work its way toward her feet, distracting her from her handcuffing fear. She looked up, saw Joseph, and shrank back toward the tree.

"Don't be afraid! I can help you! Let go of your fear and trust the Vine!"

She cringed even more.

"Fear is an illusion! Don't be afraid! I crossed it just moments ago!"

After a deep breath, she unshackled herself and lunged for Joseph's hand. He grabbed hers and the joy he felt when she was safely across filled his spirit to bursting.

He woke then, and the dream replayed vividly in his memory. Surely there was a message in it, and likely it had to do with rescuing Virginia. But interesting that he, too, was rescued. He smiled at the realization that his dream self wasn't obsessed with hand-to-hand germ combat, and the thought gave him some comfort. He hoped someday he would overcome his phobia and be able to touch people without the near panic it currently brought him. He was too tired to ponder the dream for long, however, and he slipped back into a restless slumber.

The next morning, Joseph and Virginia met in the lobby and walked together into the breakfast room.

"How did you sleep?" Joseph asked. He hoped she'd fared better than he had.

"By now Shank and Blade will be hunting us down. I'm terrified, mixed with hopeful. I haven't felt real hope in two years." She offered a wavering smile his way. "Besides, it's my birthday today and I'm giving myself a gift of courage, thanks to you."

"Happy birthday! How old?" She could be 17 like his sister the way she looked today in slacks, a white collared shirt, and a soft blue sweater. Yesterday when he first met her he'd have guessed 30.

"I'm 18."

He felt anger and fierce protectiveness surge from the pit of his stomach. Eighteen. She'd been at this for two years, so since she was 16. How could anyone force a kid into the life she'd been living? He almost wished Shank would find them so he could confront him. Then he remembered the shoulder surgery and the physical therapy that had only gotten him partial use back. His punch-throwing arm was weak and couldn't rise even to level. No, they needed to stay clear of Shank's radar. Besides, revenge wasn't his to give, but rather forgiveness. He would need plenty of prayer to accomplish that.

"Well, let's eat. I'm buying and you can order anything on the menu!"

Virginia laughed as he had intended, since the included breakfast was a cold buffet with hard boiled eggs, cereal, donuts, bananas, and oranges available. She did eat heartily, though, filling her tray with as much food or more than his.

They continued their journey toward his school, and the miles passed quickly. He talked about his studies and his plan to become a priest within a few years. She reminisced about her grandmother and some happier birthdays. He could tell how much she loved and missed the older woman.

"What happened to your mom? Do you remember her?" She hadn't mentioned her mother or father at all. If her grandmother raised her, neither must have been part of her life.

"No, she died soon after I was born. I don't exactly know how. Complications from childbirth, I think. It was hard for Grandma to talk about, so I didn't press it."

Joseph glanced at her.

Her hand rested on her abdomen almost protectively, but she continued to look straight ahead. "I wish now I knew more."

Fear shuddered its way up Joseph's spine, but he pushed it aside. No, that would be too much for either of them to be expected to handle.

A few hours later after Joseph parked the car on campus and turned off the engine, he turned to Virginia. "I have a mentor here that I'd like us to talk with. He's the one who arranged the job interview yesterday. He's been very good to me and he's wise. We need someone who has more contacts to know what services are available to help you."

Virginia nodded with hope, or perhaps the courage she'd claimed as her birthday present still shining in her eyes. "I need a place to live and a job. I appreciate all you've done, but I need to find a way to be independent and support myself."

After a pause, she shifted subjects. "Your campus is beautiful. It's been a while since I've seen such expanses of green

lawn and lovely trees." Virginia opened her door. "Shall we go?"
Hosea.

He felt the reminder in his soul. As much as he wanted to
ignore it, as much as his nervous system objected, he couldn't.
He felt he was supposed to talk to her about it. She was bound to
think he was crazy.

"Virginia, I need to tell you something first."

He watched the protective barriers come up between
them. A subtle change in her eyes and smile. A shift of her
shoulders back, as if preparing to carry a burden. He hurried to
overcome the sudden distrust he'd caused.

"I think I'm supposed to marry you," he blurted.

Virginia couldn't believe her ears. She flashed from
guarded to angry and without getting out, slammed the car door.
"Are you crazy? You think I'm going to wrestle my freedom
away from one guy simply to give it up to another? And you!
You're supposed to be a minister! A man of God! You think
marrying a prostitute will help that goal along? Germ-nutty is one
thing, but crazy is another." She wished she had slammed the
door after getting out instead of before. The car suddenly seemed
too small and she felt trapped.

Joseph held up both hands. "No, no, I'm sorry. I didn't
handle that at all well. Please, just listen."

She crossed her arms, but she didn't bolt. Where did she
have to run to, after all?

"Remember when my radiator overheated and I came to
see if you were OK?"

She nodded. Of course she remembered. It was only
yesterday.

"God sent me to you."

She rolled her eyes. Just when she thought she might have
a chance at a future, the guy who instigated it suddenly thinks
God talks to him. "Why would God send you to me?"

"He wanted me to rescue you from that Shank guy."

"That was Blade, not Shank. Shank makes Blade seem
harmless." She wondered at her own words. Shank was never
sadistic with her like Blade, but the evil that emanated from him

34

made her shiver just at the thought of him.

"Sorry. From Blade, but from Shank, too. He said I should be your Hosea."

She'd known a Hosea once. An elderly man at her grandma's church. He always smelled of mothballs. "What do you mean?"

"Hosea was a prophet in the Old Testament. God told him to marry Gomer. Remember your Gomer Pyle thoughts while you were praying?"

"I wasn't praying. I gave that up. I was talking to Grandma." Crazier and crazier, she thought.

"Gomer was a prostitute."

"Gomer was a guy prostitute?"

"No. In the Bible Gomer was a woman. God wanted Hosea to marry her to symbolize that the Israelites had prostituted themselves by turning to other gods."

Joseph looked like this made perfect sense but it made no sense at all to her. "Why would God want one of his prophets to marry a street girl? And you think he wants you to be my Hosea, to marry me? Why would I have any interest in having a husband after what men have done to me? No way am I ever going to want to have sex with you!"

Joseph looked aghast. "No! Nor I with you!"

His words crushed her. Yet again, Virginia felt filthy. Too dirty for someone like Joseph to ever want. It made her furious with every man who'd ever touched her, leaving the residue of their lust behind, marking her in a way that would let good men know she was unworthy. Would she ever overcome the pain of how men looked at her? Evil men seeing her as something to use temporarily, like a beer can to slake their thirst and then crush and throw away. Good men seeing her as contaminated and untouchable.

She felt the tears begin to burn her eyes and more anger rose. She hated to cry! Particularly in front of men! She hunted in her purse to find a tissue to wipe away the offending moisture.

Joseph offered her his container of antiseptic wipes and she took one. The scent cleared her senses a bit. She wiped under her eyes, and the disinfectant fumes stung. She blew her nose, the wet wipe feeling less than satisfactory. But she managed to take a deep breath.

"I'm so sorry, Virginia," he said, his voice soft. "I'm doing this all wrong. I didn't mean I wouldn't want to make love to you. You are beautiful and within a marriage to you, I'd feel honored to worship God for his creation of you. You are very appealing."

She didn't believe him, of course, but he was nice to try to cover up his admission.

"I mean I want to offer God my celibacy as a sacrifice and gift when I'm ordained."

Celibacy sounded pretty good to her right now, too. Could women promise celibacy to God? It must be something nuns do, but it didn't seem like most women get much choice in the matter.

Joseph continued with more caution and tenderness in his voice. "I think God has plans for you and for me. I think those plans involve us marrying. I swear having sex—I mean, making love—to you is not my expectation. Not because you aren't desirable, but because I want to only experience oneness with God, not another person."

Virginia relaxed. "As crazy as you sound, you're sweet, too." She turned toward Joseph. "Thank you for your proposal, Joseph. But no, I don't want to marry you. I don't want to trouble you for much longer." She released a long, slow breath. "Let's just go talk to your mentor and see if he can help me, without a life commitment from either of us."

"Father Bud Morris, I'd like you to meet Virginia." Joseph realized he didn't even know her last name. And she didn't give it. He had proposed, but couldn't even introduce her fully.

Father Morris stood and offered his hand, grasping Virginia's in both of his and then motioning them into chairs across the desk from him. Joseph wished a handshake could be so simple a courtesy to him. The priest hadn't offered Joseph his hand, fully aware of his contamination issues.

Father Morris picked up his pipe. "I've heard from Bishop

Walters already. Tell me how things went from your perspective. Or was there something else you two wanted to talk about?" The priest leaned back, sucking a bit on his pipe mouthpiece. Joseph knew there was no tobacco in the pipe. Since the priest had broken the smoking habit more than a year ago, the pipe served more as a prop.

The bishop. Strange. Yesterday that job was his only concern. Today it paled in comparison to the problem of Virginia.

"I assume I didn't pass inspection."

"Correct, sadly. What happened? You were a perfect fit." The priest's eyes avoided glancing at Virginia, which told Joseph he already knew what happened and the "what" sat right next to him.

"I guess God wanted me to help Virginia more urgently than the bishop's young adult program." He quickly related the story of the radiator boiling and how he stopped near Virginia. "God told me to go to her."

The priest set his pipe on the desk. "Virginia, how long have you known Joseph?"

"Since yesterday."

"If any other student of mine said God sent him to you, I'd dismiss it as overactive imagination, or because you are so pretty, wishful thinking. Joseph possesses a keen commitment to his faith. He prefers avoiding contact with people, however, so I know this prompting didn't come from him. If he says God sent him to you, I commend him on his obedience because he never would have gone to you otherwise."

Joseph sat stunned. Would he not have gone to help a crying woman if God hadn't sent him? Truth be told, no, probably not. Yet, he didn't like hearing Father Morris say it and even worse, knowing it to be true.

"There's more," said Joseph. He didn't dare look at Virginia. "He told me to be her Hosea, too."

Father Morris sat back in his chair, almost as if he'd been pushed. He cleared his throat in a long rumble that Joseph recognized from class as a delay while he thought.

"Hosea as in, rescue her from…" His glance apologized to Virginia. "From the streets, or Hosea as in marry her?"

"I think he wants me to marry her."

Virginia blew out a breath, raised her shoulders, and leaned forward. "Not going to happen. Father, I came here hoping you could help me. I need a place to stay, some kind of work to do, and a chance to support myself honestly. Can you help me with any of that? I appreciate Joseph getting me away, but that's enough. I want to take care of myself, but I need assistance getting started."

The priest nodded. "Are you a minor?"

"I'm 18, thank God. Foster care got me into all this."

"I apologize, Virginia. I'm sorry if I've made you uncomfortable today and even more sorry for all that has happened to you. I'll call the Sisters over at the Mercy Convent and see if they can put you up while we figure out how else to help."

She sat back. "Thank you."

Virginia looked relieved. Joseph could imagine that a convent would sound heavenly to her, if only for its lack of men.

He expected to feel relief as well, but he didn't. God was helping find a place for Virginia, but Joseph knew God wouldn't change what he wanted from him, if it really was that he should marry her. He waited while Father Morris called and planned with the nuns. When he was off the phone, the priest picked up the pipe and chewed a bit on its mouthpiece, then leaned forward and pointed it at Joseph.

"Go get Virginia settled at the convent. They're happy to have her. But then come back. We need to talk."

Virginia sat on the bed in her tiny convent room, overcome with how her life had changed in twenty-four hours. Yesterday morning while hurrying back from the grocery store for Bessie, she never would have dreamed that today she'd be tucked away safely anywhere, but in a convent felt beyond ironic. What a difference one person can make, and did make in her life. Granted, Joseph was an odd duck, but he'd followed what he believed were promptings from God and he'd saved her.

Perhaps it was the quiet calm of this religious house, but the thought struck her: Was it God who saved her? Had God finally seen her need? She remembered the cool darkness of the church yesterday. She hadn't prayed, really, she'd just talked to her grandma. Maybe Grandma talked to God for her? Still, that would mean he listened and answered. But why now after two years of pleading?

Because of her baby, of course, she thought. He'd helped, not for Virginia—she knew she didn't deserve it—but at least for her baby. He'd reached down and sent Joseph and saved her from Shank. The possibility brought a warmth that spread from her chest and sent tingles to her fingers and toes. God cared about her sweet innocent baby and wouldn't allow Virginia's past to ruin her baby's chance at life. Maybe he understood she hadn't chosen the life that had been forced on her.

She thought of Joseph's story of Hosea and Gomer. God hadn't sent Hosea to save Gomer, but as a message to save the Israelites. She could accept he wasn't saving her, but rather her baby.

"*Thank you, God,*" she whispered. In the deep silence around her, it seemed right to whisper. "*And thank you, Grandma.*" Beyond those words her thoughts lifted and her emotions rose, pure gratitude that became praise and filled her with joy.

A soft knock interrupted her praise, but not her joy. She stood and opened the door.

"Welcome, Virginia." A small dynamo of energy swept in. She was dressed in the same black and white habit as the sister who'd escorted her from the door to this room, but where that woman had embodied all softness and gentleness, this one emanated activity and determination. "I'm Sister Margaret. I'm called Mother Margaret here, since I'm taking my turn as head of the convent. Father Morris called me, and I told him we'd be delighted to have you as our guest."

At that moment, the first nun returned with a tray set with tea for two. She smiled and silently set the tray on the desk near the bed.

"Thank you, Sister Angela. What a kind gesture." Mother Margaret filled both cups, handed one to Virginia, and then settled herself in the desk chair. Virginia sat back on the bed and turned to thank Sister Angela but the woman had left as quietly as she'd come.

"Virginia," Mother Margaret took a sip before continuing, "your story is your own and you are free to share it with us or not. However, the more we know of your needs, the better we can serve you."

What should she say? How much should she disclose about the last couple years? She couldn't have told her story to Sister Angela for fear of shocking the gentle soul, but something about Mother Margaret suggested the woman would not be easily surprised. She hoped she wouldn't be easy to disgust either. The women in this convent lived such pure lives, so different from hers.

"I want to be totally honest with you, Mother Margaret. This room, this safety you've offered me is the last place I deserve to be." She realized her cup was quivering and rather than spill her tea she set the cup and saucer on the desk. She dropped her voice. "For the last two years, I've been a prostitute."

Mother pursed her lips, only momentarily, then nodded as if she heard such words every day. The smile that followed, one completely empty of the judgment she thought she had glimpsed, encouraged Virginia to continue.

"I didn't choose the life, other than by running away from a foster brother who raped me. You might say it was out of the frying pan and into the fire." Tears threatened to rise, which surprised Virginia. This certainly wasn't a new story for her to tell, though she didn't often share her shame. She hurried to offer happier thoughts. "Yesterday a young man stole me away from that life, saying God told him to help me." She didn't want to go into his belief that he was supposed to marry her. She didn't want to cause Joseph to sound foolish to anyone.

"Praise God for sending you help!" Mother didn't seem to think it was at all unusual. But then, Mother hadn't dealt with hundreds of men who could have helped and didn't.

"I do praise him! At least, that's exactly what I was feeling when you knocked. I had given up on God. I know I'm not worth his help, or he would have kept this all from

40

happening."

"Dear Girl, have you ever heard the story of the Good Shepherd?"

"He left the flock to find the one lost sheep?"

"Yes, that's the one! Usually sheep stay together by nature, so really, that lost sheep hadn't been very cautious. But the Shepherd didn't say, 'Serves him right. Good thing I have ninety-nine more.' He left the ninety-nine to find the one. You, Virginia, are precious to him. We might not understand his timing, but we can trust he will rescue us from evil or stay at our side throughout our troubles."

Mother Margaret had finished her tea and stood to pour more. "Is there anything else you'd like to tell me?" Her tone of voice held no accusation, but Virginia imagined Mother could see into her and already knew there was more to the story.

"I'm pregnant."

Mother's features softened and she beamed. "New life! Congratulations!"

"The baby gave me courage to leave. I'd have been forced into an abortion if the pregnancy became known."

"Then you've saved a life just as surely as the young man saved you. God bless you, my dear!" Mother Margaret set her cup down, empty again. "So, we need to find you a job, locate a place to live once you leave here, but first and foremost, arrange a doctor visit. How far along do you think you are?"

"I don't know. My clothes were getting tight. I haven't been sick. I'm not showing much yet, I don't think. Maybe a couple of months?"

"We have a dear friend, a licensed mid-wife, who visits our neighborhood clinic once a week. Tomorrow is her day, so let's get you in to see her. After that we'll tackle what kind of work you'll be able to handle."

A soft bell tolled somewhere distant in the large house.

"Time for vespers." Mother Margaret stood and collected the tea tray and Virginia's cup. She was halfway out the door when she said, over her shoulder, "Come, dear. Join us in prayer and then we'll have dinner."

Virginia followed realizing that, for the first time in more than two years, she was safe and cared for. She wasn't with Joseph, whose license plate number Shank would be able to trace. She knew it wouldn't last, but for today, there was no way he or Blade could find her. No way he could hurt her baby.

Joseph drove back toward campus from the convent. The sister who'd met them at the door had calmed his worries simply with her serene smile. And Virginia had seemed very relieved to be welcomed at the convent. He had to admit, he felt more relieved than he should. For at least a while he wouldn't have to worry about Virginia and what God had asked him to do for her. He prayed his mentor Father Morris would shed light on his dilemma.

Back at the school, Joseph waited for another student to finish talking to Father Morris. He felt ashamed of the mess he'd made of the interview Father had arranged for him. Two days ago, he'd been fairly assured of a job with the bishop's new young adult program. Now he had no idea where his future was headed. Personally, it would be fine with him if he could go off into the wilderness and pray for the rest of his life. That didn't seem like a bad calling, but Father Morris insisted he needed to work with people.

Of course, he was probably right. God had blessed Joseph's life and he should be willing to help others in return. Still, relating to people seemed to become messy so quickly. And not simply for the germs involved, but the differences of opinion, the failing to love, the reluctance to follow God's will.

The last thought accused him of his own aversion to obeying God's direction. Could it really be true God wanted him to marry? Not only to forsake his intention to live a life of celibacy, but to marry a woman who'd had countless men before him? Everything about it seemed to run counter to the path he thought God was directing.

"I don't want to get married!" The words tumbled out of him before he'd even closed the door to Father Morris' office.

"No one at this instant is waiting for you to say, 'I do,' Joseph. Calm yourself. Sit."

He did as he was told, but also squirted his sanitizer into

42

his palms and rubbed. He hated door knobs and the unknown but ever-present germs they carried.

Father Morris shook his head in a rare show of judgment.

Joseph stowed his sanitizer back in his pocket with a quick, "Sorry, Father."

"Did you get Virginia situated at the convent?"

"Yes, she seemed quite relieved."

"As, I'm sure, are you." Father reached for the pipe, but must have changed his mind. He eased back in his chair.

Joseph studied his shoes. "I'm sorry about botching the interview you arranged for me."

"I would have loved to see the look on Bishop Walters' face when he found you in the car ready to hand money to Virginia."

Heat rose to Joseph's cheeks. "And she wasn't dressed anything like she is today." The image of Virginia leaning forward with her cleavage... He forced the thought out of his mind. "Thank you for finding her a place to stay."

"Not that we've solved the problem of Virginia, have we? And the problem of you needing a job? Or believing you are supposed to marry her. You know, sometimes you can be as over-scrupulous about your faith as you are about germs. Joseph, are you sure?"

"I am." Joseph heard the disappointment and resignation in his own words.

"You know between Mercy Convent and myself, we can help Virginia get established, right?"

"God wants more from me than that. More than walking away once I know she's settled."

Father Morris cleared his throat with his pondering rumble. "You are supposed to become a deacon in a few days. And once a deacon, you are not allowed to marry, by church law."

Joseph foresaw his future priesthood slipping away. "I know. I need to choose between my ministry and what God has led me to believe is his will. Father, the most important thing in my life is to follow God's will."

Father Morris reached for the pipe and chewed on its

stem. Several minutes passed while neither spoke.

Joseph sat up straight. "Married men can become deacons." He knew that many deacons in the church come to that state as married men. Their wives needed to agree and if a wife died a deacon could not remarry. Yet even as his hope rose, another thought shot it down. Neither could married deacons become priests. A few married ministers of other faiths had become priests after converting, but that was another matter.

Father set the pipe back on the desk. "Yes, Joseph, but married permanent deacons must be at least 35 years old."

At only 26, even that option was closed to him. Was God testing his resolve to remain celibate his whole life by placing Virginia in the way? Or was he testing his willingness to follow God's will, rather than his own?

"Father, do you have a sense of what I'm supposed to do?" At the moment, he simply wanted someone else to tell him the next steps he should take. But even as he asked, he knew that he alone held responsibility for his decisions, at least for now, until he vowed obedience to his superiors as part of his ordination.

Father Morris wrinkled his forehead, then took a deep breath. "I haven't told you yet about the rest of my conversation with the bishop."

Joseph knew Father Morris wouldn't make decisions for him, but fought disappointment with how his friend had evaded his question.

"Did you hear about Father Cronin's heart attack?" Father Morris seemed to be jumping from topic to topic.

"No." Joseph wondered where this new line of conversation was leading. "Is he all right?"

"He survived, but he'll need weeks of recovery and possibly retirement."

"I'm sorry to hear that, but—"

Father held up his hand to stop Joseph. "The bishop needs to find a temporary replacement for Father Cronin. He doesn't have a priest free to transfer and frankly, he's seriously considering consolidating two parishes, but he doesn't want to further upset Father Cronin's parishioners with that thought quite yet."

"What does this have to do with—"

Again, the priest's hand stopped Joseph's question. "I suggested that you could step in as parish administrator temporarily. At least until Father Cronin is back or the parish is consolidated. I must warn you, Guardian Angels is not an easy, docile parish. Father's heart attack can likely be attributed to the stress he's been under from conflicting factions. But then, you've survived a battleground once before."

The wheels of Joseph's mind raced and yet spun in place on one word. *No! No! No!* Running a parish was years beyond his abilities. Certainly not a parish that had already caused the collapse of one leader. How did it help with Virginia, and God's seeming direction to marry her?

Father Morris read his mind. "It's a temporary assignment. It gives you time to figure out your next step."

The pieces fit together all too well. Only God could have orchestrated the timing of this option. He remembered the verse from Romans, "We know that all things work together for good for those who love God."

But how did Virginia fit in?

"Pray about it, Joseph, but don't take long."

Chapter 3

A phone call startled Joseph awake. He normally rose each morning at 6:00 a.m. precisely, but when he looked at his alarm clock it said 7:15.

"Hello?"

"Hi, Dear, did I wake you?"

"Mom, what's up?" As he became more fully awake he bolted upright in the bed. His mother and sister would arrive today to visit before attending his graduation and, *Heavenly Father, they expect to see me ordained a deacon! What do I tell them?*

"I'm just letting you know we are ready to leave the house but we heard the flight is running 30 minutes late. We'll see you at your airport! I'm looking forward to it, and Joseph, I'm so proud of you!"

When he'd hung up, he sank back to his pillow. Not only didn't he know how to tell his mother about his change of plans, he didn't even really know what those plans were. He might soon receive a different sacrament entirely, trading Holy Orders for Matrimony.

He slid out of bed and onto his knees. *Heavenly Father, I want to do your will. But I'm frightened that I'm getting it wrong. I believe you sent me to Virginia. I believe you told me to be her Hosea. Do you really want me to marry her? I'd be giving up becoming a priest. I don't understand. Please don't let me get this wrong. If I'm supposed to marry Virginia, could you convince her of it? Then I'll know it's your work. I'm not trying to test you, I simply don't trust myself.*

Blade sat parked a half block from the address where his source at the DMV said the license of Joseph O'Keefe was registered. It was one of those suburbs with uppity homes and large yards, all fussed over and showy. He opened his car door to go pay Ginger's guy an early morning visit, but then two women came out with suitcases, lifted them into the car trunk, and drove away. Good. Fewer witnesses. After they had been gone five minutes, he knocked on the front door. When no one answered, he slipped his knife along the door jam. No deadbolt. He was in within seconds.

He wandered the house, and as always when he entered such homes, he was angered by how different his own had been. He and his brother deserved to have grown up in a place like this with nice things, all in order. He looked at the family photos on the walls and mantle. Everybody smiling and all so perfect looking. The two women—several years younger but definitely the same two he saw leave the house—wore sappy grins. The teenage boy in the family photo was a younger version of the man who took Gin away, he was sure of it. The pompous dad wore a police dress uniform. That wasn't good. He'd have to be more careful than usual with this john. He laughed at the thought of informing the dad where his oh-so-holy son in the minister collar had been and what he'd been soliciting. He wished he had taken a picture of him with Gin. He would have added it to the family photo gallery.

Blade wandered through more of the house without finding a lead to where his Gin might be now. He pocketed a few niceties as he went. It was only fair. Gin wasn't making her quota today or yesterday, no thanks to one Joseph O'Keefe.

Upstairs were three bedrooms. The largest had only women's clothes in the closet. The cop dad was either dead or had flown the coop. A police badge lay near another photo of the man and a pistol was in a nightstand drawer. They might come in handy. Nothing much in the way of jewelry, but he took a pearl necklace. The next bedroom didn't seem lived in but was obviously the john's boyhood domain. Would he and Shank have been different if they'd had rooms like this? What made the john deserve this and not them? Nothing was worth taking here, but he broke the Jesus figure off a crucifix for the simple pleasure of it.

The next room was a girly light purple. One shelf was lined with cheerleading trophies. Another with framed certificates for teen service to a church. He smashed the glass of one frame against the corner of a desk. He wished he could have a go at the girl, maybe bring her to The House and show her how much harder life could be.

When it was clear this home wasn't going to give him the information he needed, he slipped out the back door and walked around the block before returning to his car from another direction.

Peace settled on Joseph after his prayer. God would clear the way if he really wanted Joseph to change direction. He didn't know how he could make his mother understand, when he didn't really understand it all himself, but he deeply believed God would not leave him to muddle through the next few days alone.

He stood up and headed for the bathroom. His cleanliness routine would take more than an hour by the time he'd made it through the tooth brushing, shaving, and bathing rituals that had weighed him down since soon after the ambush. Then he'd begin his physical therapy exercises. Maybe today he'd be able to raise his right arm a bit above his shoulder, though after four years of trying, he didn't have much hope.

He prayed as he brushed his teeth three times; as he shaved, first with a blade and then with an electric razor; while he sanitized the sink, toilet, and door knob; while he wiped down the mirror, frustrated that he could only reach the top with his left hand; and prayed more as he showered. He read Morning Prayer, and then the day's Mass readings. Eventually, he reached a peace about the offer to have him lead the stricken priest's parish.

After Mass with the other seminarians, he called the bishop, thanked him for the offer, and accepted the position.

"I'll need you to start Tuesday morning," the bishop said. "You have the theological training you need, but frankly, leading Guardian Angels Parish is going to take the skills Father Morris assures me you acquired in the military on the battle field. It's a contentious parish and I'm not doing you any favor to assign you there. You'll be doing me one if you can handle it long enough for Father Cronin to return, or for me to consolidate it with Blessed Trinity. But I don't want you to let that possibility slip out. I'm still praying about it. God help you, Joseph. You'll need it."

"Thank you for your trust, Your Excellency."

"Speaking of trust, what ever happened to that girl, Joseph?"

He felt his gut jump. "God's still leading me to help her, but for now she's staying with the Mercy Sisters at their convent."

"Be careful, Lad, very careful."

Joseph needed to return to prayer to calm himself after the conversation with the bishop. At least now he had employment to tell his mother about.

He began packing his belongings. It didn't take long. Few non-essentials fit in a seminary room. Leaving out only what he would use in the next few days, Joseph stood several boxes and suitcases in the corner, then left to meet his family's airplane.

He waited nervously for their arrival, not knowing how he could explain the change his life would be taking. Always before when he had been hesitant to tell his mother something, he counted it a pretty clear sign that he should reconsider. Yet, this time he must follow God's expectations even if they would not be well received by his mother. His sister's response he could predict. Anything that sounded the least bit romantic would thrill her. She'd be ecstatic with the idea of her hermit brother meeting and wanting to marry a woman.

Did he want to marry Virginia? Her face came to mind

and it made him smile. Not the made-up appearance he'd first seen, but the freshly scrubbed face she'd worn since then. He then pictured her looking away from him in his car, her hand rested gently on her stomach. A shiver ran up his back, but at the same moment he spied his mother, and next to her Meg, a younger version of the same slim body, thick brown hair, and dancing eyes.

After a firm embrace, his mother stepped back and beamed at him. "How's my almost-deacon, soon-to-be-priest son doing?" But as wide as her smile had been, it disappeared. "What's wrong? I can see it in your face. Something's wrong."

He noticed the wedding ring his mother wore on a chain around her neck. His father's. How he wished his dad could be here to talk to. He'd always gone to him for advice. He turned and bear-hugged his sister in what he hoped was not an obvious attempt to avoid his mother's question. "Hey, Nut Meg."

"Hey, JoJo, I've missed you," she said. She gave him the same look as her mother. "What's up?"

"So much has happened in the last few days," he said. "We need to talk. Let's get your luggage, though, and then we'll visit over lunch."

But what would he say? *Gee, Mom, after years of preparation, I've changed my mind. I've decided to get married instead of becoming a deacon and maybe a year from now, a priest.* No, that certainly wasn't going to go over well at all. *And oh, by the way, she's been a woman of, what, ill repute? But don't worry, she doesn't want to marry me.*

God help him, he was going to need pure inspiration to find the right words. He raised his eyes to heaven. *A miracle would be nice.*

That same morning Virginia walked with Sister Angela to the neighborhood clinic. Fascinated with her companion's serenity, Virginia commented, "You must love your life at the convent, Sister. It seems like a heaven to me."

"No place on earth is paradise, but yes, I'm very happy here. I don't want you to get the wrong idea, though. The convent struggles with all the same challenges and failures that any group of strong-minded women will face living together. We're not angels, by any means."

Virginia laughed. "It seems like you are to an outsider. I've been living with a group of women myself and I doubt you experience the pettiness I've dealt with."

"We're human, Virginia." Sister Angela sighed. "In our community of twelve women we've faced what feels like more than our share of challenges. Some came from abusive childhoods, two have been raped, and one has spent prison time. One sister who passed away recently had survived the Holocaust. Sister Bernadette was married and came to us after her husband and children died in a car accident."

"I'm amazed," said Virginia. "Such joy glows in your house!

"God is good. He honors our fragile attempts to love each other and we find countless reasons to be thankful. For instance, we praise him that he brought you to share your story with us, and we're thankful your friend Joseph helped you out of your captivity."

She held the door for Virginia and they entered the clinic together. "And we're very blessed to have Midwife Manda serving our clinic. She'll take good care of you. Ask her anything. She's amazing."

Before long Virginia sat in a hospital gown in an examination room, having given samples of blood and urine. A middle-aged woman with short grizzled curls knocked and entered. Her hair reminded Virginia of her grandmother and she liked the woman before she even spoke.

"I hear congratulations are in order, Virginia Shea." She shook hands with enthusiasm. "My name is Manda Brook. My friends here call me Midwife Manda. Now let's see how baby is doing and how far along you are."

Virginia's eyes filled with happy tears. If not for Joseph she might be in a very different type of clinic right now, losing the little life inside her that she already loved. Instead she felt cared for and—something else—respected. She'd missed that feeling more than she realized.

After the midwife examined her, Virginia asked, "Is

everything good? Is the baby all right? Can you tell how far along we are?"

Manda Brook grinned at her. "One question at a time. Everything seems normal, but the blood and urine tests will tell us more. It looks to me like you are about 16 weeks." She scrubbed her hands and returned to her rolling stool. "Now, my turn, and then you can ask me more. I see you came in with Sister Angela. Is the father not in the picture?"

Virginia's heart lurched, but she took a deep breath. "I've been a prostitute for two years."

Manda looked at her chart and when she met Virginia's eyes again, hers flashed anger. "You just turned 18?"

"Yesterday."

"You weren't a prostitute. You were a child who was caught up in human trafficking and I thank God you were rescued. You were victimized, but you are no longer a victim. Do you hear me? You are a survivor and you should be proud of surviving!"

Her passionate words soothed Virginia's heart like salve on a burn. "Thank you."

"You need to say it. 'I'm no longer a victim, I'm a survivor.'"

Virginia repeated her words, self-conscious that she could be heard from the next room.

"Louder, with strength and courage!"

"I'm no longer a victim! I'm a survivor!" Something burst and disintegrated within her. Perhaps shame, her long-time companion. Something else took its place and glowed warm and whole. Dignity.

"You're a mother now, and you should be proud that you found a way to protect your child. I was right when I came in. Congratulations are in order indeed!"

Virginia could feel her smile stretch and reach her cheekbones.

"Now just a few more questions to get some background. Virginia, what do you know about your birth? Did your mother tell you about it? Did it go smoothly?"

"My mother didn't survive. I don't know if she died

during the birth or a few days after, but I know my grandmother brought me home from the hospital. She was all I had. And I guess I was all she had left, too."

Midwife Manda's eyebrows had lifted. "Do you know if she had prenatal care? Did they suspect there would be trouble? I want to be sure we are prepared if there is any hereditary problem with your pregnancy."

"I doubt it. Money was tight." She hurried to add, "Not that Grandma Ruth wouldn't have done everything she could for my mother. She always did for others before herself. All the way up until she died."

"She sounds like a wonderful woman. She raised you? Did she not talk about your mother or your birth?"

"Grandma's eyes teared up if I asked questions, so I didn't. I didn't want to hurt her."

Virginia watched the midwife make some notes but then look up with a smile of encouragement. "Go have lunch with Sister Angela. Come back in a couple of hours and your lab tests should be back to us. Then we'll know more."

After Virginia had dressed and returned to the waiting room, Sister Angela stood. "What did I tell you?"

"You were right. She's amazing!" Virginia walked out feeling like she'd left "Ginger" behind and had become a new woman.

Three hours later, the receptionist directed her to the midwife's office. She took a seat across the desk from a more tired looking Manda Brook. In fact, she seemed to have aged ten years.

"I have bad news. I'm sorry."

Joseph set the bags from the cafeteria on a picnic table. This wasn't a discussion he wanted to attempt in a restaurant, so he'd chosen this park and they'd settled under the shade of a large maple tree. The heat wave had passed and a breeze felt like a blessing. Distracted, he thanked God for the beauty of the place.

His mother and sister sat on the bench across from him. "Spill the beans, JoJo," Meg said after he'd finished the blessing. "You look like I feel whenever I need to confess to Mom."

Where to start? Maybe the job would be a good introduction. "I didn't get the Young Adult Group position. Instead, the bishop has asked me to step in and be a parish administrator while their priest recovers from a heart attack."

His mother raised her eyebrows. "That's a huge responsibility. He must regard you highly."

"Not really. I botched the interview. But Father Morris talked him into this other position. Frankly, I don't feel at all qualified."

"It's certainly a lot to ask of a deacon," agreed his mother.

"Well, that's the other thing. I won't be ordained a deacon after graduation. I've been offered the parish assignment partly because I need time to reassess what God wants me to do."

Most mothers might explode. Or argue. Or show some reaction. But his didn't move a muscle. Meg glanced from their mother to Joseph. When their mother didn't speak, Meg asked, "You're having second thoughts?"

He nodded, then directed his attention back to his mom. "Are you OK?"

"I was married to a policeman. I don't surprise easily. And I certainly don't react until I hear the whole story."

"Is it a girl? I bet he's found a girl!" His sister wasn't helping. Or maybe she was. She had given him an opening he couldn't avoid.

"I met a young woman named Virginia."

"I knew it!" Meg took a large bite of her sandwich and looked very pleased with herself.

His mother, on the other hand, hadn't touched her food yet. She reached across and laid her hand on Joseph's. "Is it serious? This seems sudden. You haven't mentioned her before."

He told them the story of his encounter with Virginia and what had happened since then. He didn't spare them the facts about what she'd been selling when he first saw her crying on the street. He had to admire his mother. Apart from a few nods to show he had her focused attention, her body language remained as controlled as her facial expression.

He told her about God's leading him to help Virginia and his belief that God wanted him to marry her. Then he stopped and

54

waited.

"Joseph, I've been very proud of you and your preparation to become a priest," his mother said, "but I want you to know that I'll be proud of you no matter what work you choose. Your dad would be proud, too. I know you joined the Service in his honor and every fiber of my body wanted to talk you out of it, but I wouldn't."

"She cried, though, the night you told her, and when you were sent to the Middle East, too," Meg said.

At the time, he hadn't let himself think about how she must have worried.

"That was nothing compared to my fear when I learned you'd been wounded," his mother admitted. "Thank God you've recovered fully from that."

She didn't need to know about the limited use of his shoulder, but yes, he thanked God, too, for his recovery. He'd survived—close buddies of his hadn't—and he'd been able to return to this country and start a new phase in his life, thanks to the chaplain who inspired him to ministry.

His mother wasn't finished but she seemed to choose her words carefully. "I've admired your faith and how you've sought out God's will and worked toward the priesthood. At first, I was afraid you were doing it for me, the way you'd become a soldier for your dad. But you wouldn't have lasted this long if you weren't called to it, I don't think."

"I sure didn't think you'd make it this far," Meg said between bites. "But you've changed in good ways. Well, except for the germ thing. Or is that any better?"

He cringed a bit. "No."

His mother ignored the interruption. "Joseph, I can completely believe God urging you to help that poor girl. And how wonderful that you were able to get her out of that life. But you do tend to take things further than necessary. Are you absolutely sure God wants you to marry her? Maybe he simply was prodding you to rescue her. Maybe you're making assumptions you don't really know are true."

He desperately wanted her to be right. He wanted to believe he'd already satisfied what God wanted. Virginia was safe now in the convent and the good sisters would help her start a new life. He calmed a bit. His mother was a voice of reason. She'd always been the practical one in their home. She was spiritual, but moderated by levelheadedness. Maybe God was speaking to him through her.

Joseph remembered his request that God keep him from making a mistake. If God wanted Joseph to marry Virginia, he'd asked that God convince her. The last time he'd talked to her, that didn't seem very likely. The thought released his tension a bit more. "You could be right, Mom. I'll have to figure that out."

He was running out of time. Baccalaureate Mass was today, graduation tomorrow, and ordination the day after that. Would Father Morris even allow him to become a deacon, now that he'd declared to him that he was sure he was supposed to marry Virginia? He wasn't sure about God's intentions. In fact, he doubted the marriage expectation as strongly now as he had believed it yesterday.

"Let's go meet her!" Meg said. She'd finished her lunch, but neither Joseph nor his mother had started theirs.

His mother picked up her sandwich. "My thoughts exactly, my dear!"

"I have bad news. I'm sorry."

The words stole Virginia's breath away and she grasped the arms of the chair she sat in. She knew it had felt too good. She didn't really deserve a break, but for a short few hours she'd felt like God might have been smiling down on her anyway.

"What do you mean?"

The midwife sighed. "You are feeling well? You said you haven't been nauseous. Any bleeding? Are you particularly tired?"

"No. Why?" Virginia's stomach and chest muscles tightened. "Please, tell me."

Manda looked down at the file on her desk, but Virginia could tell she wasn't reading it.

"Well?"

The midwife looked straight into Virginia's eyes and held her gaze. She took a deep breath. "Your preliminary mouth swab test came back with a problem. You tested HIV positive. More bloodwork, a confirmatory HIV test, will be sent out to a lab to verify the diagnosis. I will get it back in a few days, but this one is said to be 98.5% accurate. I'm very sorry."

"AIDS?" She felt sucker punched.

"Not AIDS, but its precursor. Assuming the second test confirms this—it takes a few days—"

She paused, and Virginia knew she was letting the words have time to register. Strangely, though Virginia would have expected to reject the news, or fight the diagnosis, or ask for a second opinion, she didn't. She had become an expert at separating herself from fear, anger, pain, and sometimes desperation. Her mind did so now, even without her conscious effort to withdraw.

She knew she should be feeling the midwife's words deeply. Instead she sat almost emotionless. Perhaps the news confirmed some deep suspicion that Virginia hadn't allowed to come to consciousness. After all, how could she have been a mother? Not just that the effects of the last two years would keep her from being good mother material, but she'd never experienced having a mother. Her grandmother had been wonderful, but was that enough to prepare her to be a good mom? Probably not.

She half listened to the midwife's talk—something about new medications prolonging life—but she couldn't focus. It wasn't that she was afraid to die. She wasn't worried for herself at all. She was thinking of her baby. If she were to die from AIDS, who else did her baby have to rely upon? No known father. No loving grandmother willing to step in and take over.

That was, assuming the baby would survive! Would her baby also be HIV positive? She interrupted whatever the midwife was saying.

"Will the baby be safe? Is my baby affected? Will it be?"

Grandma, how did this happen? When? And how many men had she exposed since she contracted this? She had insisted protection always be used—most men didn't need convincing—but then again, the protection hadn't kept her from conceiving. Something had drastically failed. *Grandma, help me!*

Again, she missed the midwife's answer but blurted out, "I'm not letting anything happen to this baby. Even if it means I don't make it. I want him or her to live. I'll do everything you tell me to, but if there's any hope for the baby, that is our first priority. Do you understand?"

Manda sighed and nodded.

Virginia walked past a park on the way back to the convent from the clinic and longed to enter and sit in the sunshine to think. She scanned the street for the familiar cars Shank's henchmen drove even though the city was hours away. Might she really be free of him, or would she always need to check over her shoulder like this? A shiver shook her shoulders and she quickened her pace. Once inside the convent, however, the calm that pervaded the home lessened her fears. She made her way to the bright little chapel with its orderly rows of pews, desperately needing time to think.

She sat away from the windows. Though it was unlikely Shank's men would have followed her to this town and even more unlikely they'd be scanning every window for her, she wasn't going to take any chances. She had a baby to protect. Virginia hadn't come here to pray. Her diagnosis had convinced her anew that the last two years had severed her direct line to God. However, she knew no one would interrupt her while she knelt in the chapel.

Grandma, can you hear me? Did you hear what the midwife said? It might not be long before we're together again. If you are in heaven— What am I saying? Of course, you're in heaven. Grandma, can you talk to God for your great-grandchild's sake? Another church came to mind and Virginia recalled asking her grandma to talk to God to help her get away from Shank during Joseph's interview. Inhaling sharply, she realized anew that Grandma Ruth had come through for her. Here she sat, safely away from the life Shank had forced upon her.

She bowed her head, and this time she did pray. *Thank you, Grandma, and thank you, God. You did answer me! I asked for help, and you sent Joseph, and he got me away from danger. I had stopped thinking you cared. Thank you!* Her eyes filled with

58

tears but no one could see them, so she let them fall.

May I ask again? Even if I don't deserve your help, please help my baby. I'll accept not surviving, though I'd really like you to forgive me so I can come to heaven and be with you and Grandma, but even if I don't deserve that, my baby deserves a chance at life.

Her worries became more concrete. How am I going to manage a pregnancy, when I might not be healthy enough to work? When I'd endanger anyone who helps take care of me? It was one thing to die early, but another to ask people to risk their own lives if they cared for her. How could she do that?

The memory of Joseph telling her he was supposed to marry her came to mind. Joseph, the germaphobe who could barely eat his hotdog because she'd touched the bun? No way could Joseph deal with HIV. If the situation weren't so desperate, she would have laughed.

Would the nuns let her stay five more months while she waited for this child's birth? It would be so unfair to bring disease into this place of purity and hospitality. Midwife Manda's description of what steps would need to be taken to avoid contagion came to mind. She rejected the thought of endangering the sisters.

Joseph's concerned eyes and gentle ways once again filled her thoughts. *God, are you trying to tell me to say yes to Joseph? To marry him and burden him with my needs? He's supposed to become a priest! He can't be saddled with a diseased wife. Or be left to raise a baby without me.* But the likelihood that her child would at least eventually be raised by someone else remained irrefutable. Joseph would make a good father. She couldn't help but grin. He certainly would keep the baby safe from germs!

Only an hour earlier she had heard her own death sentence, and yet she could smile at the thought of Joseph changing a diaper. It didn't make sense, though nothing since her grandmother died had made sense. Neither did the calm she now experienced. Still, a realization, an absolute trust that God loved her baby did make sense. How could she doubt he would continue to watch over her and her child? He had, after all, sent

Joseph to her when her need was greatest.

She stood to leave the chapel with a lighter heart than when she'd entered it. Feeling inexperienced in such matters of faith, Virginia decided she would get a second opinion from Mother Margaret before making any decisions.

The office door was open, but Virginia knocked lightly on the door frame.

"Virginia! I was hoping you'd stop by. What can I do for you?"

Mother Margaret had been frowning at a laptop computer, which seemed out of place to Virginia. Somehow, she didn't expect modern conveniences to be part of a convent. But the room reflected the practical all-business impression she'd had of this woman from the beginning. Not only was there a computer, but a printer, a photocopy machine, and other equipment Virginia didn't recognize besides.

"Am I interrupting? I can come back later." She really hoped to talk now, while the sense of God's blessing still glowed warm inside her.

"How did the doctor appointment go?"

The question should have been enough to end the sense of God's providence, but perhaps her skill at detachment was part of his grace. "Good news, and bad, unfortunately. That's what I'd like to talk to you about."

The nun closed her laptop and turned toward Virginia, her body language and her words saying, "I'm all yours." She motioned for Virginia to take the chair across the desk from her.

Virginia related the news the midwife had given her, about her diagnosis and the possibility that her baby would be infected.

"I'm terribly sorry, Virginia. Are you contemplating ending the pregnancy?" Sister's voice held concern, not judgment.

"Absolutely not! I'll do everything I can to bring this baby alive and well into the world, no matter what that means for me. But there's more."

So that the reverend mother wouldn't worry about the danger to her fellow sisters, she hurried into the story of Joseph's belief that God wanted him to marry Virginia.

"I was kneeling in the chapel, and it seemed to me God brought peace to my soul when I considered accepting Joseph's proposal. But I've only known him a matter of days now and so I wanted to talk to someone who knows about God's ways. Could he really be leading me to marry a man who is almost a stranger?"

"Let me get this straight," said Mother Margaret. "In the last few days you've been rescued from prostitution, been proposed to, found out not only that you are pregnant, but that you are HIV positive. Virginia, how can you be sitting so calmly across from me? That alone seems a miracle."

"Or maybe I'm blessedly numb." She shook her head. "Is it denial? Shock? I don't know, but of all of it, the most amazing part is realizing God cares about me, even after all that I've done—"

"All that's been done to you."

"That too. I'm filthy in some people's eyes,"—she remembered the smell of antiseptic in the car when she'd returned to Joseph from visiting Bessie—"but God still reached out to save me."

"Virginia, God amazes me again and again. Yes, he's present in our churches and in lovely hymns and beautiful acts of kindness, but he's also ever-present in the darkest, most deprived places in this world. I'm sure he was beside you every moment, helping you survive all the pain you've endured. And I know he's holding you right now, treasuring you as his beloved."

The tears that stung her eyes were reflected in those that rose in Mother Margaret's.

"Thank you, Mother. I'm beginning to realize you might be right. But what do you think about Joseph being called to be my Hosea, as he put it?

At that moment, a nun Virginia hadn't yet met interrupted. "Pardon me, Mother, but Virginia has some callers waiting in the parlor. The young man said his name is Joseph O'Keefe."

"Perfect," Mother Margaret answered as she stood. "I'd like to meet this Hosea of yours."

***

Joseph rose as Virginia and one of the sisters came into the parlor. He introduced his mother, Mrs. Moira O'Keefe and his sister Meg, and Virginia introduced Mother Margaret. Virginia looked different somehow. He read calm and determination in her face that he hadn't seen before. She wore a tan knee-length skirt and white shirt, clothes any mother and sister would approve.

The same nun who had met Virginia and him at the door yesterday brought tea and cookies on a tray, but didn't stay.

"Joseph, I hear you've asked Virginia to marry you," Mother Margaret said as she motioned him to sit.

The woman gets right to the point, Joseph thought. "Yes, at least I told her I believe God might want me to marry her," he hedged.

"And how do you feel about this, Virginia?" asked his mother.

"At first, Mrs. O'Keefe, I thought he was crazy, and it probably sounds crazy to you, but things have happened in the last few hours that make me think God is behind this. I definitely wish I were meeting you under different circumstances. You, too, Meg. And I wish I'd met Joseph under extremely different..."

Virginia blushed and looked down at the teacup she held over her lap.

Joseph rushed to put her at ease, though her words had panicked him a bit. *Was she changing her mind?* "I'm sure we're all caught a bit off balance, but whenever God intervenes in people's lives, it must take everyone by surprise. Just two days ago our lives were headed down totally different paths."

"I thank God for changing my path," Virginia said quietly, "and for you, Joseph. I'm sorry if meeting me might detour you onto a track you never intended to take. I think you'd make a very dedicated priest."

Yes, she certainly did sound like she had changed her mind. Just when he'd been leaning toward changing his mind, too, thinking maybe he wasn't supposed to marry, but simply rescue her. Yet he'd asked God to convince her, if that's what God wanted, and it seemed he had. Joseph's grip on his teacup had grown progressively tighter and his pulse quicker. In fact, his head suddenly began to... or was it the room? Something was spinning. He stood. Mistake. He reached out to steady himself against the chair.

"Joseph?"

His mother's concern made him take in a deep breath and balance his weight on both feet. He blinked to clear his vision, then took another deep breath, which he released slowly. He felt better, though embarrassed to see everyone looking at him with concern.

He set down his cup and dodged their questioning looks. "Virginia, we are on our way to my Baccalaureate Mass. I thought you might like to come with us and visit with Mom and Meg at dinner afterwards."

She seemed relieved and agreed, then excused herself to get her sweater.

"She's a dear girl," said the Reverend Mother. "I hope you'll find time to talk alone with her Joseph. She has challenges ahead you should know about." She turned to Joseph's mother. "Mrs. O'Keefe, it's been my pleasure to meet you. I hope if I were in your place I'd appear as calm as you do. But I suspect my mind would be battling with the desire to protect my son and follow God's will at the same time." She headed for the door, and then turned. "Meg, if you ever want to consider being a sister, come visit us! Now please excuse me." With that she left in a flurry of black and white.

After a moment of silence, Joseph's mother spoke. "I like her."

"Virginia?" Joseph and Meg both asked.

"Reverend Mother. And if I'm not mistaken, I'd bet she's been in the military at some point in her life."

Joseph began to ask what she thought of Virginia, but the girl appeared in the hall outside the door of the parlor.

"I can't wait to get to know you both better," Virginia said, with such genuine enthusiasm in her voice that Joseph doubted it would be long before his mother and sister were fans.

Meg linked arms with Virginia, so Joseph and his mother followed them out to his car, but not before his mother shot him her one-eyebrow-raised look. What did she mean by that?

Chapter 4

Virginia and Meg exchanged stories about high school while they rode to campus. She truly liked Joseph's sister and looked forward to knowing his mother better. Mrs. O'Keefe seemed like a calm, practical woman, whom no one would blame if she'd gone into mother-bear mode. She hadn't. She'd treated Virginia how? "Gracefully" described her demeanor well. Virginia pondered the word. Full of grace.

Joseph apologized that he needed to join the other seminarians but would return to them after the Mass. They found seats among the folded chairs arranged outdoors on a large grassy expanse, and she settled between his mother and sister.

After a pause in conversation while they waited for the Mass to begin, Virginia asked, "Has Joseph always struggled with germs?"

Mrs. O'Keefe sighed. "No. Surprisingly that started with his work as a medic, or maybe with the ambush."

"He mentioned he was wounded while serving overseas."

"Yes, he'd been there a few months when it happened. His platoon was ambushed and his friend lunged between him and a sniper. He took three bullets meant for Joseph."

Meg continued, "Joseph pulled his buddy up onto his back and ran. He was almost to safety when he was hit."

Mrs. O'Keefe nodded. "It could have been so much worse. I thank God every day that the bullet hit his shoulder and not his heart."

Meg said, "He'd lost several friends that day before he was hit, though. He tried to patch them up, but they didn't make it. It must have been awful. I think that's what really destroyed him."

An image of Joseph falling with his buddy on his back made Virginia shudder.

"PTSD," Joseph's mother added. "Post-traumatic stress disorder, the doctor called it. Not the terrifying dreams and depression that it causes many, but this obsessive, compulsive contamination phobia instead. Maybe it was the medic training and the emphasis on blood-borne diseases, or maybe it was the gore he dealt with when treating the injured. We talked to some of the men who fought with him and it sounds like it hadn't started when they knew him. But it certainly was entrenched by the time he came home from the hospital."

Meg added, "That's when he became so spiritual, too. It all happened in the hospital."

Virginia nodded. "He told me the chaplain's example there started him thinking about going into ministry."

Mrs. O'Keefe whispered as the music began, "Which leads us to this moment."

Virginia relaxed into the beauty of the readings, the responses, the choir-led hymns, and the reverence that surrounded her. Father Morris gave the homily and talked about the new phase in life that each graduate soon would initiate. She met the priest's eyes occasionally and felt he spoke directly to her, too. For most of the young men and women here, this phase marked the first of many stages of their adult lives. For Virginia, unless God had another miracle in mind for her, this felt like the beginning of her final chapter. The thought still didn't bring her the depths of sadness it should, and maybe would soon. Instead it fortified her. She would stay strong, knowing she could endure anything for the sake of this sweet child she carried.

She rested her hand over her stomach. A movement next to her made her glance at Joseph's mother and realize she had watched her protective gesture. Mrs. O'Keefe's eyebrows lifted in question and Virginia answered with a tentative nod. Her possible future mother-in-law smiled lopsidedly in response and then rested her arm around Virginia's shoulders with the very slightest squeeze. Such a sensation of protection and acceptance flowed through Virginia that it warmed her whole body. No words had been exchanged, but Virginia sensed she had found a mother.

At a moment that Meg called the Kiss of Peace when everyone was shaking hands and saying, "Peace be with you," Mrs. O'Keefe asked, "Does Joseph know?"

Virginia shook her head.

Mrs. O'Keefe glanced at Meg, who had her back to them as she shook others' hands. "How far along?"

"Sixteen weeks. I just found that out today."

"I like the idea of being a grandmother." Then Mrs. O'Keefe embraced Virginia. "I didn't understand what would make you agree to this God-arranged marriage, but now I do. If you choose to marry Joseph, you have my blessing. And happy Mother's Day a few days late, by the way."

Mother's Day? Yes, she supposed she qualified now. "There's more you don't know," whispered Virginia.

Then Meg turned back toward them and the Mass resumed with much still undisclosed. But Virginia breathed another prayer of thanks, believing only God could have convinced a mother to accept the unexpected, sudden marriage of her only son.

Joseph returned to them as he'd promised, as soon as the Mass finished. After congratulatory hugs, his mother surprised him by saying to her daughter, "Let's walk around campus a bit and give Joseph and Virginia time to talk." She turned to Virginia. "We'll be back in about a half hour."

Confused, Joseph followed Virginia to a bench in the shade. "Is everything OK? Did you and Mom and Meg get along all right?"

"I love them both already," Virginia responded. "But no, not everything is OK. We need to talk."

They sat, and Joseph waited while Virginia gathered her thoughts.

"I went to the doctor today. Well, the midwife, actually."

He swallowed. Had he suspected? Yes, but he'd prayed he was wrong. "You're pregnant?"

"Sixteen weeks."

His first thought jumped to how messy babies are, all drool, and urping, and dirty diapers. The urge to spray his sanitizer rose, simply thinking about them. Then he realized she awaited his response. "Um, congratulations? I mean, how do you feel about this?"

Her face registered disappointment in his words but she answered, "I suspected. I'd taken a pregnancy test and had just seen the results when you met me. That's why I was crying."

"You didn't want to be pregnant." That was understandable under her circumstances.

"It wasn't that. I didn't want the baby to die. Shank would have forced me to have an abortion. I can't imagine myself being an 18-year-old mother, but I'll do anything to protect this little life."

Shame washed over Joseph. His response had been all about himself and his phobia. Hers had been selfless protection of a vulnerable, God-given life. How could he imagine himself worthy to be a priest when he didn't respond with love for the most innocent of people? He pled God to forgive him and, as he had begged countless times, to remove his germ compulsion.

He wanted to respond to people like Virginia did. He'd heard the affection in her voice when she'd talked about her Grandma Ruth and her friend Bessie, and seen the love she offered to his mother and sister. Even with all that had been forced upon her, she still opened her heart to strangers. He did not.

God, teach me to be like Virginia. Open my heart to your beloved children.

Virginia took his hand and he flinched, but didn't pull

away.

"There's more," she said, and you need to know this before we decide to marry. If you change your mind after I tell you this, I'll understand completely."

He looked into her gaze and braced himself. What worse could she have to say?

"Joseph, I tested HIV positive today."

He jerked his hand away from hers. AIDs. The ultimate blood-borne disease he'd spent his military service careful to protect himself against. Right here, right next to him.

But then he looked at Virginia and noticed the hurt he'd caused. He regretted his knee-jerk reaction and tried to reach out for her again, but she'd wrapped her arms around her chest.

"I'm sorry," he said. "I didn't mean to do that."

She had turned her whole body away. She spoke without looking at him. "It's too much to ask, I know. It would overwhelm anyone, but especially someone who struggles with contamination the way you do."

He hung his head. Even after he hurt her, she still showed concern for him. Only seconds earlier he'd asked God to teach him to love like Virginia. He'd requested God convince her to marry him, if that was what God really wanted. Well, obviously, God had responded. Now Joseph needed to show he trusted God to direct his life. He needed to obey.

As much as when he'd ridden out on missions into enemy territory, it took every milligram of his courage, but he drew this gift of God into his arms. "Virginia," he said into her hair, "will you do me the honor of marrying me?"

When she turned and studied his face, he tried not to allow any hesitation to show there.

"Are you sure?" she asked.

"Yes. I'm sure."

Virginia, who had appeared so stoic to him even when telling him she had a terminal illness, now crumpled in his arms and wept. He started to think she would never stop crying, not simple tears, but deep, chest-heaving sobs.

Yet, when his mother and sister approached, she took one more ragged breath and then sat up. He offered her his handkerchief, which she used to dry her cheeks and blow her nose. She must have seen his repulsion when she started to hand it back to him because she shifted rather alarmingly to giggles and tossed it into the garbage can next to the bench.

She stood and hugged Meg, and then his mother. "I'm sorry about all this," Virginia said, "but God seems to want us to get married, so we will."

Meg squealed and clapped her approval.

Joseph added, "And I need to start working Tuesday, so we'd better see if I can arrange it for Monday. I think the parish will accept us better if we come as a married couple, expecting our first child."

Virginia and Mrs. O'Keefe gasped in simultaneous response, "Monday!?!" while Meg whispered, "Expecting!?!"

On Sunday, after what now seemed like an anticlimactic graduation ceremony, Mrs. O'Keefe and Meg drove Virginia to the mall while Joseph was sent off to see what he could arrange with Father Morris. In a maternity shop, they chose a navy-blue dress that would serve her well in the months to come, but also project the pretty modesty of a parish administrator's wife. They bought her several more maternity outfits as an unconventional, but much appreciated wedding gift.

Virginia would have been happy to wear the navy dress for the wedding, but her two benefactors insisted she buy a knee-length, lace-covered white dress they found in a department store.

"I don't think white is quite appropriate," Virginia said, and knew she blushed as she spoke.

"Sweetheart," Mrs. O'Keefe said quietly, "you carry no shame. You didn't give your purity away and that's something that can't be stolen. I'll buy whatever color you'd like."

Virginia cringed at *sweetheart*. Too many men had used that term without any affection. She focused instead on the rest of her future mother-in-law's words and smiled her appreciation.

Virginia found a similar dress in a very pale pink and felt much better about the choice. When she tried it on for them, Meg and her mother approved her selection because of the "rosy glow" they said the pink brought to her cheeks. Virginia returned to the dressing room and, seeing herself in the mirror, enjoyed a moment of deep happiness. Who, a week ago, would have guessed she'd be free and preparing for her wedding? Maybe all things *are* possible with God, she thought.

Maybe even healing her? No, she wouldn't ask. God had worked amazing miracles to get her to this day. She'd focus on gratitude to him for Joseph and his family. She'd entrust her baby to them. That would be enough.

A tight-chested dizziness came over her suddenly and she dropped onto the dressing room chair. After a few slow, deep breaths she felt better. She changed back into her tan skirt and returned with a smile to the ladies. She waited while each of them bought a new dress for the wedding and then, with relief, she rode back with them to the convent.

Joseph had called his mother and confirmed the wedding time for noon on Monday. He said he had convinced Father Morris this was God's will, and the priest agreed to help expedite normal procedures so he could start his new job already married and bring Virginia with him.

Virginia knew her new-found peace would be short-lived. Before she was swept away in the flurry of activity, she wanted to thank the good sisters. Their home had given her safety and rest, as well as the faith she needed to make this strange transition.

She knocked on Mother Margaret's office door.

"Virginia!" the nun said, "I was thinking about you. Please, come in."

She took a seat. "I wanted to thank—"

"You're welcome. But I'd like to ask you some questions, and I hope they won't make you uncomfortable."

Virginia braced, but nodded.

"I can't get your story out of my mind, how you were forced as a child into prostitution. You see," here she softened her voice, "I was raped while in the military."

She stopped Virginia's attempt to speak by raising her hand. "No, you don't need to say anything. It happened in a different stage of my life and I've healed since then, thanks be to God. But until I met you, the experience left me very critical of prostitutes. I simply couldn't understand how they could choose such an occupation when I knew how devastating sex without love could be."

Virginia dropped her eyes to her lap. She'd felt firsthand how judgmental people could be and how their cold glances her way could wound her deeply. She didn't want to see that look on Mother Margaret's face.

The nun continued. "But then I met you. I ask you, as a representative for all the women I've judged, to forgive me. I understand now that most women who seem to be selling themselves are not doing so by choice, but either have—or believe they have—no other option."

Virginia met Mother Margaret's gaze and said quietly, "Some women fall into the life because of drug or alcohol addictions. Some say it's to support their children, but most of them have lost custody. Many end up on the streets because they are escaping terrible situations at home. That was my story. I left after a foster brother raped me. I should have gone to my social worker. I should have asked for help, but I no longer thought I could trust anyone."

"I'm truly sorry, Virginia. Sorry for what happened to you. Sorry that our society failed you. Sorry that I judged you and others like you. I suspect God is leading me toward some way of making amends. If you think of a way we sisters can help, please talk it over with me." Her demeanor lightened. "Now, tell me about your day."

"Believe it or not, I'm going to marry Joseph tomorrow...." She related all that had happened since she left the convent parlor the day before, then the two walked together to the chapel for the evening prayer.

After vespers Virginia stood and thanked the sisters for their hospitality and told them about the wedding, inviting them to come if they wished. Sister Angela suggested she could make a cake and they could all return after the wedding to the convent for a small reception. Mother Margaret approved the idea, and even offered their chapel for the ceremony. These ladies took on the same happy busy-ness which had animated Joseph's mom and sister. Virginia shook her head. How quickly they had

72

adopted her and what amazing kindness they offered. She hoped she could pay forward the same blessings for someone else sometime. Sometime soon, she corrected herself. Who knew how much time she had left?

Joseph rose earlier than usual on Monday and then thanked God that he had. His morning ritual took longer as he lost count in the middle of routines and had to begin again. He fumbled and dropped both his hairbrush and his toothbrush and realized his hands were shaking as he dressed, not in his seminary garb, but in the new black suit he'd bought while the women did their shopping. He patted the suit coat pocket for a fourth time, relieved each time to feel the box that held the simple gold band he'd purchased yesterday. He hoped it would fit. What did he know about women's ring sizes? He'd simply bought the number that Meg told him she wore, since their hands seemed about the same size.

Perhaps he should have bought a diamond. Didn't every girl expect one? But he hoped Virginia would understand both a student's finances and his determination to live a life of simplicity. It wouldn't be a vow of poverty. That would have defined his life as a priest and he couldn't ask a bride to endure that extreme, but together they could live as examples of non-materialism. He opened the box. The yellow band looked insubstantial. Maybe too simple? Well, it would have to do. If it was important to Virginia to have a diamond, he could get her one later.

Joseph placed his bathroom kit in his suitcase and then looked around. Everything was packed and the room was clean. He'd stayed up late making sure of that. One last time, he knelt next to the bed.

Thank you, Father, for the time you gave me to study here. I ask that you bless this marriage. Help us to continue to grow closer to you as we grow closer to each other. Please guide me to become a good husband. And show me how to be as good an earthly father as possible. I don't understand this new path you are sending me on, but I accept it and will struggle to always do your will. Please keep showing me what that will is.

He stood and, after one more glance around the room, he picked up his suitcase, closed the door on what used to be, and headed for what was to come. After securing a marriage license, he knocked on his mother's motel door.

"Joseph!" She stood back and looked him up and down. "You are absolutely handsome." A sadness crept into her eyes. "I have never seen you look more like your Father. I wish he could be here today for this."

"Thank you, Mom. Me too." He took a deep breath and then didn't know what to say or do next because the single tear that escaped his mother's eye brought a burning to his own.

Meg came to the rescue. "Happy Wedding Day, JoJo!" She pulled him into the room, hugged him and then gasped at the sight of the foundation makeup she'd left on his lapel.

His mother became her efficient self, dabbed it away with a washcloth, and then they were out the door.

"Are we picking up Virginia?" Meg asked.

"Actually, she would like to have the wedding in the convent chapel. She says it feels more like home than anywhere else she knows. Father Morris will meet us there."

He added their suitcases to his overloaded car. Only minutes later, Joseph and his family were kneeling in the front row of the sunny, maple-walled chapel. He prayed much like he had in his seminary room, for grace to be a good husband and father. He also asked for wisdom and courage to handle the parish challenges ahead. Then Father Morris entered the chapel, wearing white vestments trimmed with gold embroidery. He beckoned Joseph, who stood and hugged his mother and sister before he joined the priest at the front of the chapel. His knees felt unreliable and he locked them to stand at attention.

A beautiful choir of women's voices, unaccompanied by instrument, drifted into the chapel from the rear and rose in volume as they approached with a hymn of joy. Two by two, a dozen sisters entered, each carrying a home-grown rose. An unusual but lovely group of bridesmaids, they genuflected and took their places in the pews behind the O'Keefe women.

Virginia followed them, smiling radiantly. Joseph caught his breath. Her auburn hair was draped with a white lace veil.

He'd seen some older women wearing black versions of this chapel veil, but the way it framed Virginia's face captivated him. As she drew closer he took in as one lovely image the veil, the pink lace dress, the pink and white rose bouquet, and most charming of all, her glowingly beautiful face. His heart lurched and his pulse raced, but he stood captivated. He would be this God-given treasure's husband and he would cherish and protect her every remaining day of their lives.

Joseph began to love.

As she entered the chapel, Virginia's gaze found Joseph's and she felt light-headed. In fact, she began to shake, but she paused, took three slow breaths, and then continued to walk towards him. She couldn't draw her eyes away from him. His expression reflected the sentiment she supposed every bride must want to see on her groom's face as she walks towards him up the aisle. An emotion rose in Virginia that she had thought she might never feel again. She trusted this man. And she trusted the God who had brought them together.

She wasn't naive. She knew that trouble lay ahead as certainly for her as it did for every person and every couple. However, as she walked toward this groom whom God had chosen, deep in her soul rose a confidence and peace. God brought her here. God designed this. He would take care of her and, more importantly, her child. But perhaps what surprised her most was the realization that she would know joy. In fact, joy flowed through and from her this very moment.

When she reached the front of the chapel, the Sisters' song quieted. Virginia hugged Mrs. O'Keefe and Meg. She handed her bouquet to her new little sister and placed her hand in Joseph's. With all her heart, she vowed to love Joseph all the days of her life. Even if this emotion faded, she knew the choice to love would not.

Joseph repeated the same vows and she wished she could know what he was thinking. Did he mean what he said?

The priest asked for rings and Joseph gave him hers. How she wished she had one to give him. Then she felt a touch on her shoulder and she turned. Joseph's mother handed her a broad gold band, the one she always wore on a chain around her neck.

"This was his dad's," Mrs. O'Keefe whispered.

Virginia's throat tightened and, "Thank you," was all she could manage to say.

Joseph enveloped his mother into a long embrace and his face was quite flushed when he released her. Virginia handed the ring to the priest, who blessed both. Joseph slid her wedding band on her finger while swearing his love and fidelity to her. She offered him the same vow as she guided his ring down his finger, repeating, "In the name of the Father, and of the Son, and of the Holy Spirit." Then Joseph lifted her hand to his lips and kissed it.

She realized that kiss was as close as he could come to an expression of their union and, though she had declared as avidly as he that they would never make love, a sadness intruded on her joy. She forced it aside. Between her HIV status, his germ phobia, and his desire to remain celibate for God, this would need to be enough. This man loved her, maybe not emotionally but decisively. He had sacrificed his plans for her and together they would live a life of gratitude to the Source of Love.

Then to an *a cappella* chorus of *Jesu, Joy of Man's Desiring,* Virginia and Joseph led a procession from the chapel to the dining room where cake and punch awaited.

The reception didn't last long. Father Morris handed Joseph the keys to the offices, rectory, and church of Guardian Angels Parish. A new set of anxieties accompanied those keys, but Joseph refused to focus on them. Then all four of the O'Keefe family settled into Joseph's car, his sister and mother balancing travel bags on their laps.

The sisters, gathered on the steps of their convent, sang an Irish Blessing. When the lovely melody was done, they waved to the nuns and Father Morris and drove only two blocks before Joseph pulled over, apologizing. The three women waited while he squirted a generous glob of sanitizer into his hands and rubbed vigorously. Then he pulled his wipes from the glove box and carefully cleaned the steering wheel, the gear shift, the blinker, and the keys in case the germs on his hands had contaminated them.

"Oh, JoJo," Meg said. "I'm going to start a prayer campaign that God will help you get over this germ thing. All those hugs must have been hard on you, huh?"

"I'll join your campaign, Meg," said her mother.

"Me too," said Virginia.

"Well, Nut Meg, I make it unanimous. But please include a few prayers for me to manage my new job well, too."

Soon they parked and entered the airport. Joseph lifted his mother and sister's suitcases, handing them over to the airline personnel. "We'll wait until you head to your gate," said Joseph. "The new parish isn't far from here so we have lots of time."

"Nonsense. You don't need to spend your wedding day at an airport. Let me talk alone to you, dear, and then off you go." She drew him aside, and he prayed it wouldn't be "the talk."

"I have no idea how experienced you are with love making—" she started.

"Please, Mom—"

"No, your dad would do this if he were here. Let me do this for him."

He wished he could crawl into one of the suitcases, but he would listen. He couldn't manage eye contact but he would listen. She didn't need to know about the HIV or their agreement not to make love.

She went on to talk about going slowly and pleasing a spouse and being patient and speaking up about preferences. Maybe it would have been easier to hear from his dad, but he doubted it. He really didn't want to think about what he and Virginia would be missing.

When she paused, he jumped in. "Thank you, Mom. I'll keep what you've said in mind." How could he not? The words would be burned into his memory like a brand on a calf.

"All right, dear. Be good to each other and know we are here for you if you need anything. I would be happy to come when the baby is due." With that she patted his shoulder, blew Virginia a kiss, and steered Meg away to the security line.

He returned to a grinning Virginia.

"Rough talk, huh?"

The awkwardness remained with him for several minutes

in the car. Then Virginia asked what he knew about the parish assignment and he switched anxieties. He really knew very little about what he was taking on, and what he knew did not put him at ease.

Not enough time passed on their drive for Joseph to calm down before they arrived at Guardian Angels Parish. He parked and they both looked out in silence. From his car, he could see a typical older parish, complete with a white painted brick church, brown brick school, and a third building that probably served as both the rectory and office complex. Children climbed a slide and a few more were swinging on the school playground. It appeared an evening Mass had finished and a few families still milled around visiting.

Joseph longed to drive away unobserved and return after dinner when the grounds would be empty. But Virginia looked at him with excitement and asked, "Where shall we start? Go meet those families? Check the church and see who said Mass for them? Or sneak into the rectory and explore where we'll live?"

Sneaking sounded like the best choice to him, but her tone of voice told him she really didn't consider that an option. He sighed. If only he could simply be allowed to pray and worship, not need to step out of his comfort zone and socialize. "Let's go see the church," he conceded. "We'll come back for our things."

He held the car door open for Virginia and then the door to the church. The interior coolness might have been to blame for the goosebumps that raised the hair on his arms. He decided to attribute them to that anyway. He dipped his fingers in the holy water font though avoided the water, made the sign of the cross, genuflected, and then knelt in one of the back pews. *Father,* he prayed, *help me to be a servant to this parish and lead it in a way that will bring all of us closer to you.*

He became aware then of Virginia who had followed him to the pew and knelt beside him. He liked having her there, though he had not anticipated they might share companionship in prayer. He slid a bit closer so their shoulders nearly touched and then he whispered, "Lord God, help us to learn to live together on your path. Let me be the husband Virginia needs and a good father to her baby." He corrected himself. "To our baby."

Virginia smiled up at him and the sensation of protectiveness he'd felt in the wedding chapel returned. His thoughts stopped as he looked into her eyes but a noise at the front of the church made him look away.

"Hey there, folks," a man in black with a clerical collar called, "sorry to interrupt your prayer, but I need to lock up."

Joseph stood and walked toward him. "Hello, Father. I'm Joseph O'Keefe, the new temporary administrator here while Father Cronin recovers."

The priest started to reach out his hand to shake but Joseph turned away as if he hadn't noticed. It was a maneuver he'd used before, always with a tinge of guilt. "This is my wife Virginia." He motioned for her to come forward. She reached out her hand and shook the priest's enthusiastically. His shame grew.

"Nice to meet you, Father ..."

"Father Dave Brolin. And the pleasure is mine. I must run to a dinner, but I'll be back again tomorrow to fill in. The bishop told me to expect you and you can't believe my relief. I'm off to Ireland in a few days to give a retreat. I hope you'll be able to find someone else to say Mass by next weekend." He turned toward Joseph and the handshake was unavoidable. "Nice to meet you, Joseph. Best of luck with the parish." Then he hurried down the aisle and out the door.

Joseph spritzed his hand sanitizer and rubbed away the thought of the germs. He read sympathy in Virginia's eyes and it humiliated him.

"I want to look around a bit." He turned away and, genuflecting before the altar again, made his way into the sacristy adjacent to the sanctuary. He opened and closed doors and drawers, making mental note of where items were stored. All was tidy, but the room was sorely in need of fresh paint. He played with light switches until the church itself was lit. Its walls, too, showed shabbiness. Perhaps a good washing would be enough, but he suspected the darker spots indicated where paint had peeled and chipped the last time someone had disturbed the walls.

The carpet revealed wear in the traffic areas. The altar

cloths had been neatly repaired with tiny stitches that held frayed edges in place. Two of the stained-glass windows were cracked. Obviously, money in the parish was scarce and the church building itself hadn't reached the highest priority for its use.

As he scanned his new territory of responsibility, he noticed Virginia, who now sat in the first pew, her face aglow. "Isn't it beautiful?" she asked in a loud whisper.

He looked around him again, this time trying to see what she did, rather than the work that needed to be done. The setting sun backlit one side of the church's stained-glass windows, illuminating deep reds, golds, greens, and blues, which told the stories of times when angels and people met in the Bible. The light blue walls rose to a white ceiling with designs trimmed in gold paint. He walked to Virginia and then turned around to look at the altar. Kneeling angels supported the white marble table with their wings. More painted angels surrounded the cross on the wall behind the altar and then joined stained-glass-window angels who focused overhead with upraised arms, drawing Joseph's mind to the One above.

His heart surged with praise. People had labored to create this building as an act of worship for God in his goodness. Virginia knew much she could teach him, he realized, about looking for the beauty in a difficult situation.

She looked rapt as she gazed up. How could this girl—for she seemed so young in this golden light—who was married to a man she'd only known a few days, newly pregnant, diagnosed with HIV, with no loved ones to help her, radiate such joy? The only answer could be that this woman who ironically epitomized the two things he most dreaded—the sexual immorality of the world and infectious blood borne diseases—this woman knew God intimately.

He felt unworthy.

They wandered through the rest of the buildings, Virginia smiling and oohing while Joseph became more and more concerned about the condition of the parish. The school rooms each held at least 40 antique desks.

"I wish I had my camera," Virginia said. Joseph had no

idea why she would want to take a photo, but his worries increased with each room they visited and he felt too unnerved to wonder for long.

Their venture into the basement confirmed his fears that the building was heated by an ancient water boiler. There the floors posed trip hazards with numerous places the hardwood had swollen and raised, perhaps from water damage. Joseph tried to focus on the positive. Though everything needed a coat of paint, he couldn't fault the building's cleanliness. He locked the doors behind them and then they entered the rectory.

"Lilies of the Valley!" Virginia squealed. A small bouquet of green leaves with stems of white bells waited on a reception desk near the door. A card in front of it read simply, "Welcome." It wasn't clear if flowers routinely welcomed visitors to the building or if someone had alerted staff that he would arrive that night. Joseph rather hoped it was the former. He needed time to process all that had happened that day and the last thing he wanted was to shake hands with a welcoming committee tonight.

He followed Virginia through the first floor of the old building. Several sitting rooms or offices and one larger meeting room opened off the main hall beyond the reception area. At the end of the hall a kitchen straight from the 1950s occupied the back of the house, complete with a table that would seat at least ten people. Virginia opened doors and drawers like he had done in the sacristy and turned to him. "This isn't very different from my grandmother's kitchen. Much larger, of course, but I think I can find my way around here just fine. Tomorrow I could cook you my first dinner as your wife!"

He smiled his appreciation, but inwardly groaned. He hoped the whole world wouldn't need to know that they were newlyweds, especially when it soon would be obvious how far along the baby was. Thoughts of the child brought a new wave of panic. How many things could he be unprepared to handle at once!?!

"Virginia, I'm not asking you to lie, but if we can avoid people knowing we were married today, I think it would be for the best. We'd like to keep the details of why we married to ourselves, wouldn't we?"

The smile she'd worn since the lights had illuminated the church disappeared. "Yes, of course, Joseph." She turned out the kitchen light and followed him back down the hall to the stairs.

The second floor held eight nearly identical rooms, four on each side of the hall. They found the first two rooms on the left appeared to be Father Cronin's sitting room and bedroom. The other six rooms each held a desk, an easy chair, a dresser, and a twin bed. Of course, Joseph realized, the rectory had been built decades ago when priests were numerous. A parish this size would have been home to at least three men with rooms to spare for visiting priests or seminarians.

He turned to Virginia. "We haven't discussed sleeping arrangements."

Her eyes grew wide. "No, we haven't."

"Would you like your own room? It looks like there are plenty."

"I suppose that would seem odd to a cleaning lady—they must have one, everything is spotless—or to anyone else who comes up here."

"I hadn't thought of that." Joseph had instead been calculating how long it would take to sanitize a room enough to be able to relax and sleep. He hadn't much considered Virginia or her needs. He walked into one of the rooms on the right. Each pair of rooms shared a bathroom between them.

He was thinking how much he really didn't want to share a bathroom with Virginia when she said with a hesitant voice, "I think we need to move a second twin bed into one of the rooms, but I would very much like to have a sitting room to myself."

Her timid request made Joseph wonder how long had it been since she had been able to ask for anything for herself. Of course she could have her own sitting room. Maybe this parish would bring friends into her life that she would want to invite into a space of her own. They chose to call the front room on the right Joseph's office. They could move the bed from there into the sleeping room they would share. The second room would be Virginia's sitting room. He liked the idea of being able to check in occasionally and see her during his day.

Soon he had wrestled the twin bed from his office and placed it next to the twin already in the third room. Two beds didn't allow space for much else, but it would avoid raising questions.

"That leaves us with another room adjoining through this bathroom. What shall we do with that one?" he asked, not really expecting an answer.

"I think a crib will fit in there just fine, and we can use the desk as a changing table," Virginia said.

The baby. Once again, he'd forgotten about the baby. How long would it take before the reality of this new life settled in? Would they still be here in five months when the little one arrived? He couldn't worry that far ahead. Tomorrow would hold enough to frighten him. Or tonight, he realized. God help him, how could he go to bed in the same room with this pretty girl and be able to relax enough to sleep?

When they'd returned from a fast-food dinner and retrieved their things from the car, Virginia and Joseph each unpacked their personal items into a different bathroom. He took the one between his office and her sitting room. She would use the one connecting their bedroom and the nursery.

They began to get ready for sleep. As Virginia held up the white negligee Mrs. O'Keefe had bought for this wedding night, a new sense of reality settled upon her. She was married. Married to a man she didn't know and, as nice as he seemed, still a man. Shank had seemed nice at first, too. The mere thought of Shank ran a chill up her spine that made the hair at the back of her head tingle. She refolded the nightgown, slid it into a bureau drawer, and dressed in the pajamas she'd bought while on the run with Joseph.

Yet, how could she doubt him? He'd taken her away from two years of suffering and because of it forfeited his future dream. She could relate to his sense of loss. Her future would hold no dreams. There would be little future, other than, God willing, the life of a child who would grow up knowing love. And family! She realized this baby would have a grandmother and an aunt and a father. And who knew how many other relatives? Like

Virginia, she might not know her mother, but that couldn't be helped. HIV led to AIDs and AIDs to death eventually. Like Virginia's mother, she would do all she could to live long enough to give birth to this child. And, God willing, to hold it once. This time she imagined herself cuddling a blue-blanketed bundle. Yes, a son. She'd rather not bring a daughter into this damaged world. A boy would not be used the way she had been.

Or might he? A frightened face with curls of red hair on his forehead flashed to consciousness. She tried to scrub the memory away with face washing and teeth brushing.

Virginia returned to their bedroom feeling shy and a bit awkward, but Joseph wasn't in the room. From the noise of water running, he still must be washing in the other bathroom. Relieved, she climbed into one of the beds and pulled the blankets to her chin. She had intended to wait for him, to thank him for what he'd done for her today, but more than an hour passed and she gave in and let blessed sleep bring its comfort.

It seemed a long time later that she bolted upright, panicked from a dream of running from Shank and Blade. She couldn't contain the sob that escaped or quiet her fear as she tried to remember where she was. Still confused by the sound of someone breathing in her room, she drew in breath to scream. But then a man spoke her real name.

"It's OK, Virginia. You're safe."

No johns knew her by that name. And she wasn't in her room. She never fell asleep on the job. Where was she and who…?

"It's just me!"

Whoever he was, he was coming around the bed to her side. She tried to flee but her legs were tangled in the bedding. Sheer panic seized her, causing her breathing to quicken, her heart to pound, and her mind to scream out the terror that she couldn't voice. Bound in the sheets she lay helpless, and every rape of her past became one. The only hope for sanity was to disengage and force her mind away from what was about to happen. It took all her control to gasp a deep breath.

"It's me, Joseph."

Joseph... Husband... She remembered. She crumpled and

began to cry.

She couldn't see him, but felt him sit on the bed near her. He didn't move at first but then he tentatively placed his warm hand on her shoulder. Joseph. The gentle minister who wasn't quite a minister. Now she wept for what she'd done to his dreams.

He drew her close and held her tenderly, humming a little and shushing her between measures. His hand smoothed her hair. Her tension downgraded to tremors.

"Virginia, you're safe here. No one is going to hurt you."

The tremors slowly subsided.

When she could speak again, she rasped, "I'm sorry I woke you."

"You didn't. I hadn't been able to get to sleep yet."

She calmed her breathing with another deep breath and a slow exhale. "Are you worried about your new job?"

He chuckled a bit. She didn't think she'd heard him laugh before. "Yes, that's part of it. That and having a beautiful woman asleep in the bed next to mine."

She straightened and sat back. He'd called her beautiful. And he'd spoken more like a man than a minister. Part of her glowed a bit to know he thought she was beautiful, but more of her went cold at where this might lead.

"I'm better now. Let's try to sleep." She settled her head back on the pillow, pulled the bedding up to cover her pajama-clad shoulders, and turned away from him.

"You're right. I'll need to be rested tomorrow." He walked back to his bed, but she had caught something in his voice. Regret? Resignation? Disappointment?

Before long she heard steady breathing, but she didn't move until he began to snore.

A possibility had come to her that now kept her awake. Perhaps, she had suddenly thought, perhaps it wouldn't seem so bad to be physically loved by such a man. She pushed the idea aside. Such a thing couldn't happen now with HIV.

Given his germ phobia, she knew how much self-control it must have required for him to even touch her. Much worse than the teeth-gritting handshakes she'd seen him force himself into.

She sadly acknowledged that it wasn't simply HIV that kept him from approaching her, but her past, her previous experiences of other men's lust. Still, even if he was as disgusted by her as she suspected, he had shown true sacrificial love by taking her in and caring for her, and now even holding her.

She rose and wandered through the bathroom to sit by the nursery window and look out upon the darkened alley. She had done this often back in her old life, for that was how she thought of it now. She remembered many nights watching Blade's black Jaguar with the gold trim and dark windows pull slowly beneath her and disappear into the garage below The House. She shivered a bit recalling the last time she watched it. Was it only a few days ago?

The frightened eyes still haunted her. The windows of the Jaguar had always been closed, mirroring back images, but that one night the rear window of the car momentarily rolled halfway open and from her height she looked down into the terrified face of a little boy, perhaps nine or ten years old. His gaze met hers and she drew back, not wanting to think about why he was in the car and why, under his mass of curly red hair, his face registered such panic.

Tonight's sleeplessness wouldn't allow the image to be turned away as easily as it had been that night when her personal worries overwhelmed her. Her own child, still only a suspected existence at that time, presented such impossible choices that she had blocked out the memory of the moonlit face, recalling it only once before when Bessie's eyes held the same terror.

Until tonight. Earlier, before she washed, and now after her nightmare. This time the memory of the eyes wouldn't be ignored. How had she become so detached? Why hadn't she snuck down the stairs and at least listened at a door to learn who he was and why he'd been brought to that infamous rooming house? To her shame, she realized she hadn't wanted to know. She didn't want any part of the possibility that the child wasn't safe, was facing danger even more imminent than her own tiny unborn baby.

The guilt she had buried rose to clench her stomach and snatch her breath. She swallowed down the acidic bile of self-disgust. But what could she do now? Call the police? The officers she had met in Shank's neighborhood turned a blind eye to her profession, probably on Shank's payroll, or sometimes in exchange for other "courtesies." She doubted anything would come of her phone call, other than bringing her past into her present and causing scandal and embarrassment for Joseph in his new assignment. She couldn't very well say she'd seen the boy from her window without incriminating herself.

She wouldn't hide her past for her own protection, yet she would to protect Joseph. But then, what would become of the boy?

Chapter 5

Joseph woke before his 5:00 alarm in order to be sure to have enough time to complete his morning routine in unfamiliar surroundings and still begin his office time by 8:00. He silenced the clock before it would wake Virginia. Still asleep in the bed next to his, her auburn hair spread around her on the pillow, her own wild halo. Smiling, he moved to pull the blanket over her shoulders, but stopped himself, unwilling to invade her privacy. He remembered her terror in the night and vowed to himself that she would never have reason to fear again, if he could do anything to prevent it.

When he returned from his bathroom a good hour later, the room was empty, the covers of both beds smoothed into tidiness, and the aroma of coffee assured him she wasn't a figment of his dreams. Though he usually would spend the next hour in prayer, the promise of coffee drew him down to the kitchen.

"Good morning, husband!" She stood fully dressed at the stove, separating slices of bacon into a frying pan. No, she wasn't a dream, but as the bacon hit the hot pan and sizzled, filling the room with more wonderful smells, he thought she might be his own bit of heaven.

As he did for any experience that delighted his senses, he automatically thanked God, then spoke. "You're up early. Did I wake you?"

"Yes, but I'm glad. I hoped to send you off to work with a good breakfast to help you through first day jitters." She flipped a slice of bacon. "I didn't find eggs, but I started oatmeal, which can be ready whenever you are. I don't know your morning schedule."

"I usually pray before I eat."

"A blessing? Of course. Grandma and I always did, too."

"No, I pray the Morning Office, and then study the readings of the day."

Disappointment slipped only momentarily across her face before cheeriness replaced it. "That's fine. I can keep things warm until you're ready."

He swept aside the comfort that his habits offered. "We can start new routines now that we are together. Breakfast smells heavenly. I can pray after we eat."

"May I join you then? I'm not very good at talking to God, but I'd like to learn."

He hoped disappointment didn't appear obvious before he forced a smile. His prayer time was a refuge from the discomfort of dealing with people, but how could he not be pleased with a life partner who wanted to share his faith? Still, he realized with mixed feelings that the last few minutes were an undeniable indication that his old life was over.

As he moved into her realm and started opening cabinets in order to set the table, he asked God to help him overcome his selfishness and become selfless for his wife. To sacrifice in small and large ways, like Christ did for his bride the Church.

Virginia took pleasure in the near-purr of approval that rumbled in Joseph's throat at his first bite of crispy bacon, as well as the raised eyebrows and smile when he tasted her oatmeal. After they cleared the plates into the sink, she followed him to his new office and sat across the desk from him as he read aloud the prayers and readings. She had thought he would talk directly to God, and maybe he did in the silence while they meditated on the readings, but she was a little disappointed that he didn't share that part of his prayer with her. Still, she bowed her head and tried to connect with God herself.

But who was she talking to? Was it the Father on the throne in heaven? The Son on the torturing cross in each of these rooms? Or a vague Spirit bird? She decided to address her prayers to "Grandma's God." She didn't have a mental picture of him, but could ask her Grandma to pass on messages to God, maybe like a 911 operator who could send emergency information to the right responders. Besides, she liked talking to her Grandma.

Thank you, Grandma's God, for bringing me to this marriage. To this safe place. Help me be a good wife. Her mind turned to her baby, as it frequently did now. *Help me prepare for this child, to build a strong relationship with Joseph so we can be good parents.*

Joseph interrupted her thoughts as he began to read aloud from his prayer book again. How would she ever learn to pray?

At 7:50 Joseph closed his missal and cleared his throat. "Well, wish me luck on my first day. I guess I'll know soon what I've gotten myself—I mean us—into." As he tightened his tie, a tremor quivered his hands. *God help me.* If he took time to think about it, he would have to admit his emotions were a mixture of dread and terror. He reminded himself he wasn't headed out into a battlefield, only simple parish administration. He wasn't in danger of death, other than the possible demise of his ministry career. That thought brought no comfort.

He went downstairs and arrived in time to unlock and hold the door for a young woman who parked her bicycle and hurried to enter in front of him.

She smiled her thanks and the kindness in her dark eyes momentarily distracted Joseph from his fears. Her brown hair was long and wavy, with the sides pulled loosely back with clips above each ear. He guessed she was in her early twenties. "Can I help you?" he asked.

"I'm Claire Davis." She slung a backpack off her shoulder and settled it next to the desk that faced the door. "I'm acting receptionist/secretary for the time being, but usually I'm the youth leader for the parish. Are you our replacement priest? So sad about Father Cronin. I hope he'll recuperate quickly. Not that I'm trying to get rid of you, of course. Sorry, I tend to rattle on."

She blushed, and Joseph found himself a bit tongue tied before he shook off her effect on him. "I'm Joseph O'Keefe. Not a priest—" He nearly said "yet" but reminded himself he never would be now. "I'm the temporary parish administrator until Father can return or the bishop can find a replacement.

"Hmmm. Who's going to say Mass? Father Brolin came to get us through the weekend, but he's off to Ireland. Wish I could be off somewhere, too. Maybe things would settle down by the time I got back."

"I've heard the parish has been, um, going through difficult times."

"If there are two people left who agree on anything I haven't met them in a while. Anyway, welcome. And good luck. Once word is out you are here, I suspect you'll be inundated with appointments for everybody to plead their case." Claire looked past him. "Heaven help us, here comes the first one now."

At the same time as a blustery man with heavy eyebrows and stooped shoulders came in the door, Virginia descended the stairs and arrived at his side. He'd forgotten about her.

Joseph watched Claire pull a wide-eyed stare away from Virginia and turn toward the visitor. "Sam Jorgen, head of the Parish Council, this is…" She reddened again.

"Joseph O'Keefe, Parish Administrator for the time being." He forced himself to extend his hand to Mr. Jorgen, who shook it while not taking his gaze off Virginia. "And this is Virginia, my wife." How strange the words sounded. He wondered if they came across as new to the others as they did to him.

"Morning, Ma'am," Sam said with a head dip. "Claire." He didn't smile at the youth leader before he turned to walk into an adjoining parlor where he obviously was accustomed to talking to the priest.

Joseph glanced at Claire, who nodded him on to follow Sam. He did and, with relief, heard Claire welcome Virginia and begin to introduce herself.

At noon, an exhausted Joseph saw his sixth visitor to the exit.

"Quick, lock the door," said Claire. "We take a half-hour break at twelve. Virginia is in the kitchen. I packed my lunch, but if you want I'll bring it in and join you to catch you up a bit."

He nodded in his dazed, overwhelmed state, and followed her. After washing his hands and thoroughly sanitizing them at the kitchen sink, he joined the two ladies at the table. Someone, probably his wife, had found a nice white tablecloth to cover it and a vase of garden flowers sat in the middle. Three places were set.

Claire waited for him to say grace, then sighed. "Off to a rough start?"

Virginia ladled soup into three bowls and looked at him with sympathy. "Are you all right?"

He shrugged. He really didn't know if he was. "What happened to these people? They all seem more prepared for battle than ministry."

Claire chewed and swallowed. "Money is tight and every group wants what isn't available. School parents think more should be spent on the school. Others think the school should close. Social-justice-minded people want us to do more for the poor in our area. Others want us to focus on the financial needs of our members. Some parishioners want more traditional liturgies; some want contemporary music. Some can't wait for growth; others don't want anything to change. The neighboring parish, Blessed Trinity, has a charismatic priest and a more affluent neighborhood. Parishioners are moving there, and we don't exactly have an atmosphere that welcomes new people.

"What keeps you here?" Virginia asked.

"This was my grandparents' parish. I used to love coming to Mass with them as a little girl. Everybody knew each other and all the families were of either Irish descent or Italian. Their faith flowed strong and so did their family values. When I saw this job advertised, I was ready to graduate with a double major in

Catholic Liturgy and Social Justice. It sounded like a good fit, and I jumped at it."

"What was the job description?" Joseph had finished his soup and the homemade cornmeal muffins which tasted as good as the aroma in the kitchen had smelled. Virginia brought him two more. Claire passed him the honey butter.

"I'm part-time Youth Minister, Music Director, and Social Outreach Coordinator. Mrs. Haggerty, the receptionist and housekeeper, quit the day Father had his heart attack. Not sure which came first. But I stepped in until she can be replaced so that someone would be here when people come to the door."

"Thank you for that. I can't believe you could hold all those responsibilities and be part time." Joseph was impressed with her dedication.

"Well, true, I'm pretty much here full time and then some, but I don't have other responsibilities so I'm good with the hours."

When the conversation paused, Virginia asked Joseph to save time after work to take her to the grocery store.

"You don't drive?" Claire asked.

"Not yet. That's on my to-do list, though, when Joseph can help me learn."

"In the meantime," said Claire, "if you want to use my bike during my hours here you are very welcome."

"Thanks, Claire. I'd like to do some exploring and learn about the community."

Joseph's cell phone rang as he was headed back to his office.

"Hi, Mom! How was your trip home?"

"The trip was pleasant, but getting home wasn't." Her voice had an edge to it that Joseph hadn't heard in a long time.

"What's wrong?"

"Our house was broken into while we were gone. Some things are missing, some were intentionally destroyed."

"Oh no! What kinds of things?" He imagined the television, computer, and small electronics, most likely gone.

"It took a while to figure out, but my pearl necklace, your

Dad's police badge, and his sidearm are gone, as is the picture of you I keep on my dresser. And strange things are broken. A couple of your sister's cheerleading trophies, your crucifix, and some picture frames.

Joseph couldn't help but wonder if his new wife's past was finding its way into his family's safety. It made him momentarily regret having ever stopped his car across the street from her. Then he chided himself. God's hand was in his car breaking down. He had to trust that God was in control of this, too.

"I'm sorry, Mom." His voice softened as he imagined his mom and sister arriving home to such a discovery. "Are you frightened? Should I come home? Have you've talked to the police?"

"I think we'll be fine, but thank you. The police are most concerned about the service pistol and badge, but they assume it's a random break in."

"I'm not so sure, Mom."

"No, I was afraid not, too. Meg's pretty scared. I have an appointment to get a new security system installed today."

As he hung up, three people, who obviously did not like each other, came into his office. Sam Jorgen was back, and introduced the school principal, Dr. Mary Knightly, as well as Mrs. Susan Burke, the head of the Parent Teacher Association.

"We need to discuss the school budget," Mrs. Burke said when they had all been seated. She struck Joseph as epitomizing the word matriarch, with greying, professionally styled hair, and an upward tilt to her chin that suggested either far-sightedness or disdain.

"We are approaching a serious shortfall," the principal explained. She was tall, thin, and exuded efficiency. "Unless we can come up with another $25,000, we won't be able to make payroll for June."

"I'm sorry, but as I've said before, the money simply isn't there." Sam Jorgen ran his fingers through his thinning hair. "We can't allocate what we don't have."

All three turned to Joseph, who had no answers and no idea what to say. "Um, fundraisers?"

"We've done the usual: auction, jogathon, wrapping paper sales." Mrs. Burke scowled at him. "They simply aren't bringing in what they used to."

"That's true of our Sunday collections, too," Sam Jorgen said with a sigh. "In fact, I haven't been able to pay Claire yet this month either. We'd be in even worse shape if Mrs. Haggerty, the housekeeper hadn't quit." He looked at Joseph. "I hope your wife won't mind taking over those duties. Claire is handling the front desk for the time being."

Again, Joseph didn't know what to say. He hadn't considered the exertion Virginia would need to keep up with a home as big as this rectory. "I'm sure we'll make it work," was all he could reply. "Dr. Knightly, Mrs. Burke, could we meet again in a few days? I'll work with Sam here to look over the budget, and I'll see if the diocese can give us any help."

The two women agreed and left, and Sam promised to pour over his figures again and meet soon to see what they could do together.

"But I'll tell you now," Sam said to Joseph, "I don't see much hope."

Virginia had spent her morning organizing their clothes into closets and drawers and learning more about the rectory, her new home. She had scrounged around the kitchen and felt pleased to put on a nice lunch for Joseph and Claire. She liked the secretary/youth minister but was surprised at the bit of jealousy that rose in her when Joseph listened to Claire with a crooked smile she hadn't seen before.

Claire's offer to borrow her bike made her feel guilty for her thoughts. Joseph hadn't been hers long enough to warrant such possessiveness, she told herself, and then she worried that maybe he didn't consider himself hers at all. Their marriage had come about in such a strange manner. More likely, she probably seemed more his burden than his wife.

Joseph did drive her to the grocery store, but he seemed so exhausted that she suggested he rest in the car until she finished. He was asleep when she returned, but shook himself awake and helped her load the groceries into the trunk and then into the kitchen. Virginia shooed him off to bed while she put things away, and he was fast asleep when she checked on him before going to her own bed. She turned out the lights but lay awake wondering when this place would feel like her home, and if their relationship would ever feel like a marriage.

The next day Joseph entered Father Cronin's room at the priests' convalescence home. He had brought a few personal items from Father's office, but mainly hoped to learn some coping strategies or wisdom to deal with the multiple parish controversies. The room was even smaller than his dorm room. A single bed, a small dresser, a recliner but no desk. Other than the requisite crucifix over the door, the room was devoid of any décor, lacking photos, get-well cards, and warmth.

Father Cronin didn't take much room in the bed. Beyond small, he seemed shriveled like a forgotten piece of fruit. He looked at Joseph with suspicion.

Joseph introduced himself.

"So yer my replacement? Well good luck to ye. Yer goin' to need it." The older man extended his hand and made a cross sign with it in blessing. Then he motioned Joseph to sit in the chair beside his bed.

"Ye look mighty young for pastoring. When were ye ordained?" Father Cronin's voice was high and a bit wheezy.

"I'm a lay minister. I'm the parish administrator until you are up and about again." Joseph wasn't sure from the look of the priest if that would be any time soon.

"Well, don't hold yer breath. I'm not ever goin' back to those people. Look what it got me. Nearly died."

"I was hoping you could give me advice. How do I handle all the dissenting opinions? What can we do about the budget? What were your goals for the parish?"

"My main goal became trying to keep them from killing each other or me! I can't tell ye what to do, 'cause I never knew what to do me self. I'm giving up on the lot o' them. I'm too old for this. I just want to spend my time praying and reading. That's all I ever wanted." The priest rolled over in his bed, turning his back on Joseph.

The words struck Joseph to the core. Praying and reading. That was really all he wanted to do, too. But he certainly didn't want to become as detached and angry as Father Cronin. He couldn't blame the old man. It sounds like the parish had been too much for him. But was he following in the same footsteps? Would he, left to his own devices, die in a tiny room with no visitors, feeling like he'd made no difference to the world?

On her second day, with their belongings stowed and her cupboards filled from shopping the night before, Virginia was ready to explore beyond the bounds of the rectory and see what type of community she now shared. She checked with Claire again to make sure she could use her bike and then eased onto the seat and wobbled her way to the street. But her time without a bike soon gave way to old abilities and she began to pedal with confidence.

She had memorized her address, a bit worried she could become lost and not know her way back. However, a cellphone Joseph had given her on their wedding day directed her to the address the Sisters had given her of Midwife Mandy's regular clinic, which happened to be only a couple of miles from the parish. She passed modest older homes and small retail businesses, a more pleasant type of urban neighborhood than she had left behind in her city. The streets were lined with mature trees and children's toys were scattered in the yards. When she had found the clinic, she stopped in and left a message with her cell phone number, asking for the midwife to call her to arrange for when she should be seen again. As she turned toward the door, she noticed a bulletin board with missing and runaway children posted on it. She scanned it quickly, afraid she'd see the frightened eyes and mop of red curls. She didn't, but could hardly feel relieved knowing loved ones were desperate for news of any of these children.

Back on her bike and taking a new path home, Virginia passed a police station. The coincidences suddenly seemed like something more. She guessed Joseph would say God wanted her to do something. She thought again of the child's teary eyes pleading up at her, turned the bike around, and taking a deep breath, she forced herself inside the precinct door.

The station was quieter than she expected and her entrance made a uniformed officer look up from his desk. "Can I help you?"

"I think I want to report a crime."

"You think?"

"Well, I do. I need to. It's about men forcing kids into..." She looked back at the door, wishing herself on the other side of it. "About kids and teens being made to..." She thought of Joseph and how kind he was. And how he'd asked her to not talk to anyone about her past. But she knew he wouldn't want more children to suffer what happened to her. "I was forced to be a prostitute, and I'm pretty sure there are some little boys being groomed for the same thing."

The officer's face registered sympathy. She hadn't expected that. She hadn't been sure he would believe her, but with a sad nod he motioned for her to take a seat in a small room with a desk and two chairs. "Can I get you a cup of coffee or something while I bring someone in to talk to you?"

"Just water if it isn't too much trouble." She took a seat, momentarily proud that she was doing the right thing, but then out of habit detaching herself from her emotions. She imagined herself riding the bike, heading back to the rectory, with nothing more on her mind than what to fix for dinner. Then back further in her mind, she was in Grandma's house. Grandma was making dinner for her, she wasn't pregnant, or married, or about to risk her life. She held on to the image only momentarily before a uniformed woman entered and drew her mind back to the stark room.

She had kind, but tired green eyes. She wore her straight black hair pulled into a professional bun. "I'm Detective Kate Monroe. Thank you for coming forward. I'd like to listen to your story and take notes as we go, if that's agreeable." She took a seat across the desk and opened a laptop, then waited.

The first officer brought in a glass of water, smiled at Virginia, then closed the door as he left.

Virginia took a long drink to stall for time. What she was about to do would be far worse than running away from Shank.

He wouldn't forget or forgive this, and he would make sure she would pay, probably with her life. She rested her hand on her baby's current haven. She had vowed to do whatever it took to give her child a chance at life but what she was about to do would kill them both if he got to her before she gave birth. She knew Shank had some control of his local police department, and she feared what she said here, even hundreds of miles from him, would go straight to his ears. Then the little boy's pleading face came to mind again, and she knew she had to do her part to make the world safer for more children than just her own.

She breathed out long and slow before she began. "I was almost sixteen when my Grandma Ruth, who took care of me, died. After being raped in a foster home, I ran away. But I landed in the clutches of a pimp named Shank." Uninterrupted, she told it all: the deception, the beatings, eventually earning enough trust that she was allowed to work the streets, how a young minister—she didn't give his name—helped her escape just recently. But she saved the story of the young boy for last because that was what made her feel most ashamed. Not the many men she had been with, but that she had done nothing to help the boy with the imploring eyes.

When she had said all that she could, she stopped. Detective Kate asked a few more questions, including the address of the house she had lived in those two horrible years. Then she asked for her current address and phone number. Her mind raced. She didn't want to bring Joseph into this and risk his work at the parish. And could Shank access the police report somehow to find her?

Detective Kate tried again. "How and where can we reach you?"

"Do I have to tell you? Could I just stop in here now and then in case you need me?"

"No, I'm sorry. We need to have contact information. What worries you about that?"

She told about her fears that Shank might have access to police records. The detective waited for what Virginia wasn't saying.

"And I'd like to not bring innocent people into this.

People I live with."

The detective's lips pursed and then relaxed. "Agreed, for now, how about a cell phone number. Can I get that from you?"

With relief Virginia gave her the number.

As she stood to leave, the detective stood, too, and laid a hand on her arm. "Are you safe now? Are you truly away from people who will take advantage of you?" She glanced to Virginia's baby bump and then straight into her eyes. "Do you have someone who will help you and support you?"

As she formed her answer and realized the profound truth of it, she relaxed for the first time all day. "I do."

Virginia parked the bike near the rectory front door where Claire stored it and then, back in what she realized was beginning to seem like her very own kitchen, surveyed her cabinets with a sense of satisfaction she hadn't known in a long time. The pleasure grew as she remembered baking with her grandmother in a similar kitchen in times past. She brought the flour canister down onto the counter, then grinning at the connection to her past, she gathered yeast, salt, oil, and sugar. Before long she was up to her elbows in the push-fold, push-fold of kneading dough. Her senses were delighting in a ritual she had missed for those awful two years: the aroma of warm yeast, the sound and soothing rhythm of kneading, the stickiness giving way to silken dough, and the anticipation of the taste of warm buttered bread. She even began to hum an old favorite tune of her grandma's.

Within a few hours, the rectory smelled of warm promise and happy times. Virginia could almost reach out and touch her grandmother as the scent of bread transported her back to the Saturdays when they would work together and then clean house while the bread rose. Sundays then were for church and relationships, homework and neighborhood walks. Saturdays were all about domestic arts and happy security.

When a timer buzzed Virginia out of her reverie, she pulled the first of four pans of rolls out of the oven. Down the long hallway, she heard a door open and caught sight of a young woman, head lowered, wiping her cheeks with quick fingers. The aroma must have reached the woman, because she lifted her head and inhaled deeply, looking Virginia's direction.

"Come join me for a hot roll, fresh from the oven," Virginia called.

The woman didn't move for a moment, but the aroma proved irresistible. She walked into the kitchen. "I haven't smelled fresh baked bread for way too long."

"Have a seat, I was just going to have a cup of tea." Virginia bustled, a bit unsure of where to find teacups, but opened a cupboard with mugs and figured they would do fine.

"I don't want to intrude," the woman said, but Virginia smiled and pointed to a chair and her visitor dropped into it with what might be either fatigue or resignation.

"I'm Virginia, and I'd love a good chat. I haven't met many people here yet."

"Corazon Sanchez. My friends call me Heartie, and anyone who bakes bread rolls from scratch is certainly a friend of mine."

"Thanks! Why Heartie?"

"Corazon is Spanish for heart. I guess my mother was feeling romantic the day she named me. Being born on Valentine's Day didn't hurt either, I suppose."

Virginia laughed. She added butter and jam to the table and took a seat. The woman across from her wasn't much older than she, maybe early twenties, but the sadness in her eyes made her seem older. She was a pretty brunette, all soft and round like the roll she held up to her nose.

Hearty inhaled and closed her eyes. "My grandmother used to make these, God rest her soul."

"Mine, too," Virginia said, and realized her eyes were welling. "Were you close to her?"

"I was, and I miss her terribly. It's been less than a year but still feels like I lost her yesterday."

Virginia nodded and waited for Heartie to continue. "My mama hasn't gotten over our loss either, which is part of the problem. I just graduated from college and have been offered a good job, but I'd need to move. I don't know how to tell Mama, or if I should even accept the offer."

Would she have moved away from her grandma, if things

had been different? She couldn't rewrite history enough to know, but if grandma hadn't died, she'd be graduating from high school and ready to start out on her own. She knew she wasn't the one to offer Heartie advice, but she certainly could listen and empathize. They chatted together another half hour and when they parted with a hug, Virginia felt better. Judging from the light in Heartie's eyes, so did her new friend.

"I'm going to tell my mama today. Maybe she'll move with me. We could both use a new start."

As Heartie left, Virginia's cell phone rang. Midwife Manda set an appointment for two weeks away, expressing pleasure that Virginia had moved near her regular clinic.

"You went to the police?" Joseph sighed as he sat on the bed to take off his shoes. This had been a long day of interacting with unhappy and dissatisfied parishioners. He was looking forward to an early bedtime, but it was obvious Virginia had been waiting to talk to him. Claire had stayed for dinner, and the two meetings after that meant this was the first they'd been alone since breakfast.

Virginia stood across from him, looking nervous, and he thought, like a little girl hoping she wasn't in trouble. Joseph forced himself to focus on her, rather than his desperate need to be alone and simply close his eyes.

"I felt like God wanted me to go to the police. I'm not sure, but it seemed like it."

Joseph sighed. "Well then I'm glad you did. I remember some pretty amazing things happening last time I followed his prompting and went to see if a crying lady was OK." He hoped she'd smile and relax a bit but she nodded distractedly.

"I know you didn't want me to tell anyone about my past unless it couldn't be avoided without lying. I'm sorry. And I'll be sorrier still if this causes trouble in the parish." She suddenly gave him a wild, frightened look. "Or if Blade or Shank learn it was me and find us here!"

He rose and put his hands on her shoulders. He rarely touched anyone and from her startled response, he hadn't touched her like this either. Still, it felt OK. No skin contact, that was good. Fewer germs and no unguarded thoughts wandering… He forced his mind back to the moment. "God is with us, Virginia. He's been protecting us so far. We need to trust him when we try to follow his lead that he will do his part and be with us."

She nodded and, yes, there was the smile he had hoped for. Her eyes met his, held their gaze, and he felt her shoulders relax. It would certainly be nice to lean his head down, just a bit, and maybe she'd raise her chin for the kiss he began to imagine. He dropped his hands to his side. She stepped back and looked down. They both cleared their throats and the moment passed.

He sat on the bed and she sat, too. Not near, but so they could face each other.

"What did you tell them?"

She related the conversation with the detective. As she told him about the boy who glanced up at her from the car, he shook his head. He didn't want to know, to believe that any men could be so perverse as to abduct a child for such horrendous purposes. And yet it had happened to his Virginia. He released a breath he didn't know he had been holding, and gently drew her close with an arm around her shoulders. She rested her head against him, and the tenderness of the moment healed the edges of something raw inside him. He hoped it did the same for her.

Yet, his desire to kiss her frightened him. She was so pretty, and vulnerable, and he had to admit it, he certainly found himself attracted to her. He'd have to be more careful.

Chapter 6

Joseph seemed distracted the next morning when he came down to breakfast. Around mid-morning, when she was in the kitchen deciding what to make for lunch, she heard footsteps and thumping above her. It was unusual for Joseph to spend time in their room during the day, but everything was still so new that it was strange to call anything unusual.

After lunch, when she carried a small load of laundry upstairs to put away, she nearly dropped the basket upon entering their room. Joseph's bed was stripped bare. She walked through her bathroom to where the nursery would be. Yes, the bed in that room was now neatly made and covered with Joseph's bedspread. She sat on the desk chair, confused by the sadness his move brought her.

She probably should feel relieved. He had left her with a room of her own, with doors that locked and assured privacy. They had agreed they wouldn't be intimate, and now that they knew there was no longer a housekeeper, they didn't need to keep up appearances. But the last few nights she had become accustomed to hearing him breathing near her. And it would have

104

been nice if he'd warned her. Had she done something to upset him?

She remembered then how close they had felt after their talk last night. How near to her he had stood. How it almost seemed like he might kiss her. She hadn't known if she wanted him to or not, and then he stepped back and the moment passed. Was that what brought this on? Was her HIV frightening him? She supposed kissing wouldn't be a good idea. Or was it simply her past that made him decide not to share a room?

She decided not to ask him. She would busy herself with other things. The size of the rectory left plenty to keep her occupied, trying to maintain its many rooms. The cleaning wasn't fulfilling, though, and the baby wouldn't occupy her hours for months. If her marriage wasn't going to be a source of satisfaction, she would need a project, a way to feel like she could contribute something to the world.

As the following days passed, when anyone left Joseph's parlor, they were usually met with the tantalizing aroma of baking bread. Women of all ages and elderly gentlemen often visited with Virginia at her kitchen table, their cares temporarily forgotten while they shared conversation and found a friendly ear. Young and middle-aged men were not invited to the kitchen, but instead found a wrapped half-dozen rolls waiting on the entry table on their way out. She could imagine Joseph's relief to avoid the customary handshake at the door, his hands suddenly occupied with the offer of his wife's homemade gifts.

When particularly quarrelsome meetings brought the sound of raised voices to the kitchen, she would knock on the conference room door and enter with cinnamon rolls, muffins, or raisin bread. She suspected it was physically impossible to argue while eating a sticky bun.

Joseph wished he were making the steady progress into the hearts of his parishioners that Virginia seemed to be managing. There were days when he'd prefer she were the parish administrator rather than he. At least he could sleep better now that he'd moved to a room of his own. But in truth, Virginia was finding a place in his heart as well as helping him find a place in his heart for the parishioners, breaking down his protective walls, pebble by pebble. When he complained about how frustrating Mr. Jorgen had been in a meeting, she gently mentioned he had lost his wife only a few months ago. Or when he couldn't understand why Mrs. Burke would vote down every request for money to be spent on anything but the school, Virginia knew Susan had been one of the women pivotal in building the school decades ago. She wanted it to be available when her three great-grandchildren were ready to start their education.

Dumbfounded when one girl ran out of Youth Group with tears in her eyes after he asked for help to set up his chastity program, Joseph later learned the girl had divulged in Virginia's kitchen that she was newly pregnant. Little by little he began to understand that each person who crossed his path was trying to do the best he or she could with what burdens life, and their choices, had brought their way. He realized with surprise that Virginia was teaching him compassion.

As he began to know more about this temporary flock, he would ask meeting attendees to help him understand their position by giving him some history of their individual or group contributions to the parish so that they could be shown the appreciation they deserved. He pushed each side in a disagreement to offer in good faith one thing they could give that the opponent wanted. He opened every meeting with a prayer that God bring peace to their work. He praised the good intentions and past accomplishments of each side. But even as meetings became less confrontational and more cooperative, the fact remained that money was short. They were hard pressed to compete against the neighboring parish that was blessed with higher economic levels and financial success. Remembering that the bishop had mentioned the secret possibility of combining the two parishes, he decided to request a meeting with the neighboring pastor.

"We can't beat them, and we may very well be joining them," he thought. He hoped the visit wouldn't be as discouraging as his meeting with Father Cronin.

The next morning in the parlor, Joseph slipped out of his

shoes and set them on the visitor chair, then climbed onto another chair in order to hang his diploma. Virginia had presented him with a very nice frame for it, and he wanted to please her by giving it a place of honor on the wall where guests would see it. He felt more relaxed around Virginia now that he'd moved. And he was certainly able to sleep better at night.

"That's a military spit and polish, if I ever saw one."

Joseph turned to see Sam Jorgen studying the shoes he had picked up and settling himself into the chair they had occupied. He nodded. "Army. Medic."

"Father Cronin's shoes were always scuffed. Conscientious Objector, he told me once." The man's voice held disapproval.

Joseph finished hammering in the nail and settled the frame on it. "Straight?" he asked.

"Lift the right a bit." He motioned with his head, and his voice warmed with respect. "You saw action. Purple Heart if I'm not mistaken."

"What makes you say that?" Joseph thought his physical therapy had at least gotten him to the point where it wasn't obvious anymore.

"You didn't hang the frame high enough to need a chair, unless your nailing arm isn't as good at reaching as it used to be." He looked self-satisfied.

Joseph stepped down and accepted the shoes Mr. Jorgen held out to him. "Great deductive skills. Military?"

"Army criminal investigations special agent, retired." He gave a quick salute. "At your service." He leaned back in his chair, seemingly a different man than the difficult debater Joseph had experienced in meetings. "I came to talk about the budget, but we can talk finances anytime."

Joseph sat across the desk from Mr. Jorgen and slid his feet into the shoes. When they were tied, he gave his full attention to his visitor.

"Veteran's Day came and went and we didn't do a thing about it in this parish, just like every other year since I retired. But I think that's a shame. And I think you're the man to help me put it right, maybe even in time for Memorial Day."

"What do you have in mind?" Joseph hoped it wouldn't be another draw on their almost non-existent finances.

One week later, Virginia answered a knock at the back porch. Her heart jolted in her chest when she saw the backlit silhouette of a giant man at her screen door. Her hand flew to her chest, as if to still the painful beating.

Blade! No! God, help me!

Had he already found her? She glanced behind her. She had to run! To get away! She couldn't return to that life!

"Sorry, Ma'am. I didn't mean to startle you." The drawling voice was not Blade's, and as she shielded her eyes against the low sun, she confirmed her mistake. A very large black man of the same build as her tormentor had stepped away from the door. His eyes were wide but kind, and he held up his hands to show her he wasn't a danger. "I just smelled your bread baking and it made my stomach growl. Do you have any to spare?"

Virginia forced herself to smile and clasped her hands to stop them shaking. "I thought you were someone else. Yes, of course. I'll be right back." She wondered if she should have invited him in. She didn't really know the etiquette of a church rectory, but he seemed content to settle himself on one of the yard chairs, so she returned to the kitchen and made him several sandwiches out of her bread rolls and cold chicken slices. After she let Claire know what she was doing just to be safe, she poured him a large glass of iced tea and then took the meal to him. She sat in another yard chair, one that wasn't too near.

"I'm Virginia," she said.

He nodded, but took a large bite and chewed it fast before he closed his eyes and sighed his approval. "Thank you, Ma'am. Your bread is a true gift. My name is Eugene Sullivan, but I'm none too partial to Eugene. Friends call me Griz." He downed half a glass of the tea. "Because of my size, not my disposition." He smiled and she found herself smiling back.

"Pleased to meet you, Mr. Sullivan. What brings you here?"

He had finished two roll sandwiches and was starting the

third. "I heard about a meeting for veterans at your church today. I'm early, and I wouldn't have bothered you if the smell of your bread didn't nearly drive me wild. Nothing quite like homemade bread. It's been a long time since I had any."

"Where are you from?"

"Tennessee originally. Since I've been out of the service, I've been wandering around looking for work and a place to settle."

"What kind of work are you looking for?"

"Well, that's the problem. I joined up right out of high school. I'd done plenty of hunting before that, and the army didn't take long to make me a marksman. My aim is steady and true. But there's not much call for sharp shooters in civilian life. So, I'm looking for anything honorable."

Virginia watched his eyes darken before he looked down at the ground. "I'm not doing any more shooting."

She could tell there was more story behind his words and understood it was a painful one. She connected with him on that level. They both wanted to put their pasts behind them and choose a better future. The silence between them felt comfortable, and as he ate she looked around her. She hadn't spent any time in the back yard. She sat in the shade of a large tree with broad green leaves she didn't recognize. An old single-car garage filled one side of the yard. The rest lay open to the alley.

She gestured to the house across the alley from the rectory. "Mr. Jorgen lives there." He had pointed to it when he told her about losing Mrs. Jorgen a few months ago. So much pain in people's lives.

She continued, "He's the one who came up with the idea for a veteran's gathering. Maybe there will be somebody there to help with a job search."

"That's my hope, Ma'am." He handed her back the empty dish and glass.

"I'll send my husband out when he's free with a refill on the tea, if you'd like."

He nodded and stood when she did. "I'd appreciate that. Nice talking to you, Mrs....?"

"Mrs. O'Keefe." She still liked the sound of that. "Pleasure to meet you, Mr. Sullivan. Please call me Virginia." Mrs. O'Keefe was Joseph's mother, after all.

"Yes, ma'am, Miz Virginia."

Joseph did bring the tea refill to the man Virginia told him about. Something about the size and bearing of the man brought back the image of his dream of the vine and the chasm. It predisposed him to like Griz, in spite of knowing nothing about him. Or maybe it was because of their shared veteran status, for Joseph usually felt more comfortable with men who'd been soldiers than any others.

They chatted a few minutes and then walked together to the church hall. Joseph introduced Griz Sullivan to Mr. Jorgen, and the three men moved chairs into a circle in the church hall gathering room. Soon a dozen or so men and a couple of women who'd served in the various arms of the military gathered. Two young men used wheel chairs. Ages ranged from mid-twenties to mid-eighties, but the conversation seemed to flow across the generations. Joseph watched a few business cards be handed out to the youngest veterans and saw hope rise in their faces. He also noted the elder members sitting a bit taller as they told their war stories.

Virginia entered the room and all the men stood. She carried a pan with pot holders, and from the aroma Joseph guessed it contained her delicious sweet rolls. He suspected everyone's mouth began to water like his as he jumped up to relieve her of the pan. He gestured with his head toward the counter where he headed to set the rolls down near the coffee urn.

"Come get them while they're hot!" he said, and didn't have to say it twice.

The group gathered quickly around the treat. Virginia cut the rolls and slid them onto paper plates, which barely made it to the table before they were scooped up into waiting hands and mouths. As the veterans awaited their turns at the coffee pot, they broke off into twos and threes.

Joseph wandered among the conversations, then spotted one young man in a Fort Kennedy T-shirt.

"Did you do basic training at Fort Kennedy?" he asked.

"Yeah, three years ago. You ever stationed there?"

"I did my training there, too, almost six years ago now. Is Sergeant Kao still there?"

"You mean Kick Box Kao? Yes, and going strong last I heard."

Joseph was grinning now. "Can you still kick the ball?" He hadn't thought of his basic training in a long while, but he'd never forget the sergeant who insisted his recruits learn how to defend themselves even if their arms were unavailable. He would hoist a ball on a rope up to the men's ear height. They had to practice until they could side kick the ball on every attempt. Once they could do it consistently, he'd tie their hands behind their backs and they had to learn to pivot and still kick the ball without their arms to balance.

The young soldier walked away from the others, smiled broadly, then spun and side-kicked impressively high at an imaginary ball.

Everyone stopped talking and clapped or whistled.

The young man gave a quick bow, then looked at Joseph. "Your turn?"

Joseph hadn't tried this in years, but he set down his cup, caught Virginia's eye, and accepted the challenge. He backed up a few steps before he sprinted forward, pivoted, and side kicked up into the air. It wasn't as high as the younger man's, but the group applauded his attempt, too.

"What's your name?" Joseph asked his challenger.

He came to attention, saluted, and shouted, "Private First Class Ben Santini, Sir!"

Joseph barked, "No hands, Private First Class Santini!" just as their sergeant had, before realizing what he might have gotten himself into.

But Ben nodded, clasped his hands behind his back, and ran towards the imaginary suspended ball. He pivoted and made a perfect kick, nearly as high as his first had been. Perhaps only Joseph knew how difficult the maneuver was without arms to give momentum and balance.

The group stamped and whistled their approval though,

and then turned to Joseph to see if he would try. Well, what could he do? He had to be a good sport. He had started this, after all.

He shrugged, clasped his hands behind his back, ran three steps, pivoted on his left foot, flung his right leg up and out..., and slammed into the floor, his left shoulder taking the brunt of the force. He stood with Private Ben's help and grinned, rubbing his shoulder gingerly. The onlookers, having collectively held their breath when he fell, broke into laughter and a few slapped him on the back good naturedly. It wasn't until a few minutes later that Joseph realized he hadn't felt the need to cleanse his hand after Ben had grasped it and helped him up. He walked over to the table where Virginia stood, with her hand still at her throat.

"Are you hurt?" She sounded a bit alarmed.

"No, only wounded my ego," he replied, ignoring the desire to rub his shoulder to be sure.

Then she let out the most appealing giggle and shook her head. "Boys!" She picked up her empty pan and headed out of the room.

He wished he could follow her. Instead he scanned the group. Here and there a couple of men had moved apart and sat together, including Griz and Mr. Jorgen, deep in serious conversation. He didn't know what they were saying, but he sensed this gathering had done something important.

Mr. Jorgen must have agreed, because he announced they should return and bring more veterans next week. Days ago, Joseph might have felt usurped by the announcement without his approval, but he knew Mr. Jorgen better now, and agreed completely.

On Thursday, the morning of Virginia's prenatal appointment, she joined Joseph for his morning devotions after breakfast. He had begun asking her for suggestions of prayer topics and she usually asked for God's blessing on one or another of the parishioners she had come to know. This day, though, she asked for his prayers that the appointment go well. To her surprise, Joseph sat silent for long moments before he began. Finally, he reached out and took her hand.

"Dear Father, we long for the healthy growth of this child,

and your guidance to make us good parents. Like I do every night, today we ask for a miracle. We dare to ask because our whole relationship together has been designed by your hands and so we know miracles are not impossible. If it is your will, please heal Virginia of HIV. Wash away any remnants of that disease and make her whole and strong. She is precious to me and I want her to live as long as possible. If it's not your will, give us strength and guidance to accept what lies ahead."

Virginia realized tears were rolling down her cheeks. She was precious to him. He'd been praying for her healing every night. He wanted her to live as long as possible. Even if he still rarely touched her, and never crossed the divide from his bed to hers, even if he didn't seem to want her the way she was just maybe beginning to want him, she knew and felt deep in her core that she was loved.

Still a bit dazed a few minutes later, she thanked Claire for the use of her bicycle and started pedaling toward the clinic. She had become less wobbly on the bike over the weeks, but it surprised her how quickly she became winded with any uphill exertion. Still, she was happy for the exercise and the chance to be on her own. Out of habit, she continued to be hyper-aware of her surroundings, always on guard in case she might see the cars of any of Shank's thugs.

She chided herself, reminding the old timid Ginger how unlikely it was that they would trace her so far from their city. She had left "Gin" behind and felt happy and hopeful as Virginia O'Keefe. In fact, by the time she sat in the examining room, her mind was focused on the sweet infant she carried and not on her past.

The midwife entered and greeted her like they were old friends. She perched on the stool across from the examining table where Virginia waited. "I received your bloodwork back from the lab. Give me a minute to look it over."

Virginia nodded and Manda slit the envelope and pulled out her report. The midwife scanned down the paper and Virginia watched her eyebrows lift in surprise. Before she looked at her patient they returned to a neutral position.

"What's the verdict?" Virginia tried to sound nonchalant,

but knew she failed.

"Amazing good news!" Manda's face matched the pronouncement.

Virginia tried not to get her hopes up. *Remember Grandma's God, we know you can work miracles for us. I know my baby and I are in your hands no matter what we are about to learn.*

"The second test was negative. You are not HIV positive. This really is rare, but I'm delighted for you."

Delighted wasn't strong enough a word for how Virginia felt. How wonderful for Joseph that his worst fears weren't embodied in her! Would he move back into her bedroom? She grinned and wiggled on the table. "Are you sure? Do we need a third test to really, really be sure?"

"I'm sure. This test is more thorough than the cheek swab we did at the sisters' clinic. You are HIV free!" Manda's voice convinced Virginia it was really true.

"I ran more tests than typical prenatal procedures. When you told me that your mom didn't survive your birth, I added a few more so that we'd know if we were up against some things that are hereditary. All those tests were negative!"

She would live! She could raise this child herself!

The two women grinned at each other for a moment, then Manda took charge. "Let's get on with this." The exam went quickly and the midwife answered Virginia's questions while she worked. Next, she did a breast exam, her fingers making small circles as she felt all quadrants of the left side. After she moved to the right side, she stopped mid-sentence. Again, Virginia focused on Manda's eyebrows. They tented, flattened, and then dipped into a scowl, but returned to a neutral position before she met Virginia's gaze.

"What's wrong?" Virginia asked. She felt herself detach, the wall that protected her emotions raised high.

After a deep sigh, Manda answered, "I found a lump. It's probably nothing to worry about, but we should do a biopsy just to make sure."

She should have known better than to let herself feel too much joy. It obviously wasn't meant to be that she could live a

114

normal life. Not even now that she was out of so many other dangers.

"Cancer?" The word came out monotone, as if computer generated.

"Chances are higher that it's simply a cyst. Let's not worry yet. Does it hurt when I push on it?"

"No." She could tell from the quick eyebrow twitch that was not the answer Manda hoped for. But she forced herself to refuse to worry until the biopsy results were back. She would dwell on the new, wonderful results of her HIV blood test. And she wouldn't tell Joseph about the lump until she knew more.

Chapter 7

That same Thursday evening, as Blade drove into the garage below The House, Gus was hurrying to his Jeep. Blade didn't consider the little bulldog of a man very bright, but he made up for it in loyalty. Gus came to Blade's car, so he rolled down the window.

"Dude, am I happy to see you. I didn't know what I was gonna do." Gus lifted his phone up as if to show Blade, and then pocketed it. "I just got a call that my mom's in the hospital. I gotta go, but Shank told me to make a run for him tonight. Can you do it for me?"

"Yeah, sure. What's it take?" Blade wasn't thrilled. He'd rather a good drink and a long night in bed, but if Shank needed something done, he'd do it.

"He wants me to take the new redheaded kid, Ryan, to a drop off. Says to get him at 3 a.m. sharp in Shank's room and move him while he's half asleep. Take him to 24th and Jefferson and leave your parking lights on. A guy named Hud will come and get him from you."

He'd forgotten about the redhead. It had been several

weeks since Blade had picked him up and brought him to Shank. Usually the turnaround was quicker, he figured, though come to think of it, he really didn't know what became of the kidnapped boys. He brought them to Shank and didn't see them again. He'd never been the one to take them back. Shank probably figured it was better that way.

"Ransom's been paid, or do I get it from him?"

"I don't know about no ransom, but Shank says to remind the kid again before he goes that if he talks, his mom dies. And you can't tell anyone about the drop, even the other guys. You got it?"

Blade figured Shank wouldn't be happy about Gus telling even him about it, if those were the orders, but that was Gus's problem, not his. "Yeah, I got it. You owe me one."

Gus nodded and then set off towards his car.

After a short sleep, Blade rose just before 3:00 and went to Shank's room. It was dark, and it sounded like Shank was in the shower, so he shook the boy who was asleep on the couch. "Come on, kid. Time to go."

The boy moaned and turned his back to him. Blade shook him again and this time the boy stood, but didn't look up. He was unsteady on his feet, and Blade figured he was probably lightly drugged. Good. He didn't need the kid running off. He guided the boy out into the hallway and downstairs to the parking garage. Once in the Jaguar's backseat, the boy lay down and went back to sleep.

Blade had driven only a block when a dark SUV passed him going the opposite way, followed by another. Then two cop cars. He kept an eye on them in his rear-view mirror. They were stopping near The House. Blade turned off his headlights, then U-turned and parked. Another SUV turned down the alley that went behind The House. "This is not good," Blade said aloud, forgetting the boy in the back until the kid sneezed.

It certainly wouldn't be ideal to be stopped and have cops find a drugged kid in his car, but no one seemed to be noticing him. He tried to call Shank, but there was no answer. His brother was probably still trying to get warm in one of his frequent long, hot showers. He started to dial another of the guys, but it was already too late. The cops had burst through the door of The House. Blade knew what they'd find. He knew he should hightail it out of there, but he couldn't. His brother was in deep trouble and, this time, there was nothing he could do about it. He slid over into the passenger seat, so that his car looked more like the other driverless cars parked on the street.

Blade watched his little brother Shank be dragged from the building and pushed into a squad car, hands cuffed behind him. He looked so skinny in his pajamas and without his cashmere coat. If he only could put on a few pounds he wouldn't need the coat. Then two more of the guys were brought out to squad cars, followed by most of the girls, who were led into the SUVs.

Blade tried to think of ways to rescue Shank, but before he could come up with a plan, five little boys were taken out of the building next door to theirs, some carried in policemen's arms. The sight of them hit Blade like a sucker punch. Several of the boys he recognized from when he had met them at various places throughout the city and had brought them to Shank, who assured him it was a kidnapping scheme. He'd been told the boys were returned when the ransom was paid. He'd trusted his brother, even though he'd never been part of any returns.

The truth clenched his gut, and he barely had time to open his door before he threw up in the street. Shank was doing what their mom's boyfriend had done to them. Shank, the one person in the world he'd always trusted, had lied to him.

Several men were led out in handcuffs after the boys. A couple worked for Shank but the others were strangers who wore polos and khakis or who were buttoning up business suits. He was sick again, though only bile was left. The smell brought him back to childhood, heaving in his mother's apartment, leaning over a filthy toilet. He had been sick each time after he'd been forced… He pushed the thought away.

But then the patrol car drove past him and his brother stared him straight in the eyes with a look that gave Blade his next order. Revenge. The look told him to figure out who was to blame for this and make sure they didn't live past the day he found them. He hadn't killed anyone in a long time, not since his "stepdad" turned his evil attention away from him and raped his little brother instead. The old drunk had deserved what he got, and so did whoever caused Shank to be taken away from him.

Anger grew to fury as he realized who had ruined everything. Ginger! She was still missing. She must have gotten far enough away that their usual agreement with the cops hadn't protected them. This was her fault! If she hadn't ratted, no one would be arresting his brother. His only family. The kid brother he'd protected and stood by always. And he would never have known about those boys.

Ginger needed to pay. To feel like he did right now, like his world was torn away from him. Not only his brother and his livelihood, but his last trust in anyone. He'd find her and make her wish she'd never left them. Never opened her mouth. He'd make sure she'd never make it to trial. And then maybe Shank would be released. They'd go back to normal.

Blade slid back to the driver seat, ready to jump into action. But then the boy sneezed again. The sound stopped him in his tracks. What was he supposed to do with the kid? He'd probably missed the meeting with Hud. Hud, who he now realized was not a dad bringing a ransom to get his beloved son back. He was a creep buying the kid from Shank. Ready to put the kid up to be used.

The taste of the bile in his mouth told him things would never be the same.

Still, Shank was his brother and the boss. He owed Shank and couldn't go against him.

The nausea returned. How could Shank do that? There was no denying now what had been going on in the building next door. Shank had been arranging for boys to be messed with the way they'd been messed with as kids.

Well, he wasn't going to be part of that. But what was he going to do? He wished he had his brother's smarts. If he'd been a little slower getting the kid out of The House, this boy would be on his way back to his family now. And Blade would be on his way to jail. But wherever he took the kid would be risky. Before long he'd be awake and full of questions. Best to get rid of him before that happened.

Chapter 8

Blade turned around to look at the sleeping boy. His hair was sticking out every which way like Shank's used to do when he was that size.

Blade shook him. "Kid, what's your address?"

The boy opened his eyes and glanced around him. He sat bolt upright and tried the door handle. But Blade always had the child safety locks on. You never knew when you might not want somebody escaping out of your backseat. Not in this business.

"Be cool, uh, Ryan. Where do you live?"

The boy shook his head.

"What do you mean, no? I'm asking where you live. I want to take you home."

This was met with a look of distrust.

"Look, kid. I'm sorry. I didn't know what was going to happen to you when I took you. I thought we were kidnapping you, and your folks would pay us, and you'd go right back. Honest, I didn't know the real story. So now I want to get you away from here and back home, but I need to know where you live, and you need to promise not to talk about me to anybody.

I'm just some nice guy who took you home. That's all they need to know."

Slowly the boy took a crumpled envelope from his pocket. It was addressed. The kid must have been trying to send a letter to his mom.

"This is it? Where you live?"

Ryan nodded and Blade headed toward the suburbs.

It was only 4:00 and still pitch dark when they arrived near the boy's house. Blade parked within view of the door, instructed Ryan not to turn or wave or in any way point to his car. Then he released the lock, and Ryan flew out and across the street. He rang the doorbell and pounded on the door. Before long a young woman opened the door, and the kid flew into her arms.

Blade couldn't take his eyes off them. Never in his whole life had he been hugged like that. This kid was really loved. Like he and his brother should have been. Like every kid should be. No matter what Shank said, Blade was glad he'd brought the boy home.

He could hear them both begin to cry before she pulled him in and closed the door. Good kid. He had remembered not to point to the car.

Blade backed out of the parking spot and around the next corner before he turned on his headlights and shifted out of reverse.

The kid would talk, of course, so he needed to get away. Then he would turn his attention to Ginger and revenge. That, at least, he could do for Shank.

Virginia treasured the smile Joseph still wore that Friday morning from hearing about the HIV results the day before. Once again, she had waited all day for a moment alone but at last in his room she had shared her relief. He hadn't touched her since the conversation about talking to Detective Kate, but when he heard her news he gave her a quick one-arm hug. It wasn't quite what she had hoped for, and he did wash his hands afterwards, but it was progress. And now, without HIV, perhaps there might be more touching in their future. Maybe he would even move back in with her. He slept only one room away, but the distance held a meaning she didn't quite understand.

She paused as she made her bed and tried to imagine them together in it. No. She wasn't ready for that yet. And he might not ever be. Maybe hugs were good enough.

She heard Joseph call goodbye as he left for his meeting with the neighboring pastor and had almost finished tidying their room when her cell phone rang.

"Good morning! Virginia speaking." she answered. It did seem like a very fine morning, but her muscles tensed as she realized this might be the biopsy results.

"Virginia, this is Detective Kate Monroe."

Her heartbeat drummed in her ears and she sat quickly, struggling to take a deep breath. "Yes?"

"I have some good news and some not so good."

Virginia didn't like the sound of that phrase. It felt too much like the story of her life.

"Usually we would take longer building up to an arrest, checking out your story, verifying all we could, but with children in danger, we risked some short cuts. Officials' feathers were ruffled, but we pulled it off. This morning at 3 a.m. officers stormed the address you gave us."

Virginia swallowed. Now instead of struggling for breath, she was fighting to calm and slow her breathing. She could feel a tremble start in her midsection and spread to her hands. She almost dropped the phone. As she brought it back to her ear, she heard, "They arrested Shank, as you called him, and two of his men. We took seven young women into custody. The garage under your building had a connection to the next building. It looked abandoned, but you were right about the children. We found five little boys who were drugged and locked in their rooms. We've taken them, as well as the young women, to be checked at an undisclosed hospital. They say some of the women are likely underage, too. Virginia, I speak for the police force when I thank you for being brave enough to come forward."

"Did one of the boys have red hair?"

Silence, then, "No, I'm sorry."

Disappointment gave way to fear.

"Was one of the men you arrested Blade?" She wouldn't

feel safe if he were still at large. One hundred percent loyal to Shank, it wouldn't be long before he guessed she was the informant and tracked her down.

More silence. "I'm sorry, no. Not from your description. And I'm afraid that isn't the only bad news."

Virginia couldn't respond, so Detective Kate continued. "The media has the story, and though I kept your name confidential, they know our precinct instigated the arrests. I'm really sorry. I hope we haven't endangered you. If you want, we can get you into protective custody for a while."

Still Virginia couldn't find her voice. She knew all the detective could hear was her raspy breathing.

"Please give me your address so I can send a squad car to you."

And bring her sordid past into this new hope-filled life she'd begun? No, she wouldn't do that to Joseph. She could run, leave Joseph and the parish, but then what? She needed help. Someone who could think straight. She'd tell Joseph what had happened and hope they could work out a solution together. That's what husbands and wives do, after all.

She steadied herself. "Thank you, Kate. I'm glad to be forewarned. Don't send anyone yet. That would attract attention I don't want. I'll call you when I figure out what to do next."

She hung up the phone and tried to stand, but her legs wouldn't hold her. She settled back into the chair. What would Joseph say? What would he do? She realized the answer to that question. He'd pray. She turned her thoughts to God, and though words didn't form, she offered him her fear and yearning for safety. She figured he would understand. Slowly her breathing and heartbeat returned to normal. Gradually her thoughts settled back into words. *Help me, Grandma's God. You brought me out of slavery to this good place.* She placed her hand tenderly on her abdomen. *Protect me and my loved ones.* In time, she calmed enough to think beyond her family. *Please be with the children and the women who have a chance at freedom now. Give them healing and lead them into healthy lives.*

The no-nonsense face of Mother Margaret came to mind. She made a quick call to her, and then with her permission, back

124

to the detective. Mercy Convent would be the perfect place for Shank's victims to do some quiet healing until their next path could be found. If only Virginia could climb back into that haven. Back where Blade would never find her.

Father Mike Kohler's handshake was firm and warm. As he sat in the offered chair, Joseph patted his pocketed bottle of sanitizer, as if reassuring the bottle rather than himself that he would use it soon. However, Father Kohler's ease was contagious and soon Joseph felt relaxed. The man and his office were tidy and comfortable. An elderly yellow Labrador lifted his head and thumped his tail from his bed in the corner.

"What can I do for you, Joe?" Father Mike turned to take two bottles of water from a small office refrigerator and handed one to Joseph. He leaned back in his chair, seeming totally relaxed and open to whatever this meeting brought. "How is Guardian Angels treating you?

"Fine, thanks" He corrected himself. "Actually, things aren't fine. Not that they are treating me badly. I'm trying to find my way as I go, not having any experience in administering a parish. I was hoping for some advice."

"I can't imagine taking on a parish when I was fresh out of seminary. New priests usually have plenty of on-the-job training from the series of pastors they help before they are ever given such heavy responsibilities. You've really been thrown into a challenge." His understanding smile softened words that could have sounded patronizing. "This must be very difficult for you."

Joseph felt at ease and he decided to speak freely. "Father Kohler—"

"Please, call me Mike."

"Father Mike. I'm not a warm person. I'd like so much to exude welcome and openness the way you do, but it isn't in my personality. I don't think I have a grain of extroversion in me. I dread the beginning of every day and then feel guilty for not loving my parishioners the way I should. I see now I was never meant to be a priest." He briefly told Father Mike about the sudden change of direction God had required of him in the last few weeks, without mentioning Virginia's past.

"But I do want to help this parish and be a blessing to them. How do you do it? Can you give me any wisdom or pointers? How do you maintain your cheerfulness when opposing factions start treating each other like enemies? Or when there simply isn't money enough to implement the dreams—reasonable, valuable dreams—that would truly bless the parish?"

His host smiled. "How do you avoid being like Father Cronin, carried out on a stretcher from trying so hard?"

He hadn't imagined that years of thwarted effort might have caused Father Cronin's bitterness, but Father Mike had, and suddenly it was obvious to Joseph that he had misjudged the older priest.

"Yes."

"Joseph, imagine you are out on a hike and stumble across a newborn fawn who is limping and has been abandoned. What would be your first impulse?"

"I hope I'd pick it up gently and get it some help." He didn't mention how he'd have to overcome thoughts of lice, or ticks, or bacteria in order to do so.

"You might be bitten or kicked if you did. But I try to see each of my parishioners that way. As fawns. Well, actually as lambs, but that's a bit cliché." He directed Joseph's attention to the Good Shepherd painting—a smiling Jesus carrying a lamb across his shoulders—that hung above the chairs for his visitors.

"Each person is wounded and may very well try to strike out at me when they need help the most. I must be patient and help them get what they need anyway. That's what God asks of me. To love his lambs. Often loving them in general is easier than liking them individually. And notice, God doesn't ask me to make them love me, or even like me. He simply wants me to love and help them."

"You like your work."

"Tremendously. There's nothing I'd rather do."

"Thank heaven for priests like you. The Church and the world, we need you."

"God has a plan for you, Joseph. He'll put you right where your skills allow you to do the work he has for you."

Griz Sullivan and his job search came to mind. Was

Joseph himself in the same situation as the weary vet, trying to transition to a new way of life?

"Well, I hope I'm brave enough to follow that plan when I figure it out."

Before Joseph left, Father Mike offered to say Mass at Guardian Angels in between the two services at his parish every Sunday. Perhaps he knew of the Bishop's plan for the future, but then again, he was simply the kind of man who helped wherever he saw a need. It certainly would ease Joseph's burden of staffing every Mass each week.

Though Joseph left feeling completely inadequate compared to charismatic Father Mike, the priest's words buoyed him. God would place him where he needed him and with God's help maybe he wouldn't do more harm than good.

He felt so relaxed that he didn't want to return to his office and its challenges quite yet. He decided he might as well stop and get his car registry and license updated to his new address.

When he had finished at the Department of Motor Vehicles, he drove home. A sense of gratitude sent him into the church before returning to the rectory. After genuflecting, Joseph knelt in one of the back pews. He thanked God for Virginia's reprieve from the HIV diagnosis, for the promising work with the veterans, and for how well his meeting with Father Mike had gone. As he concluded his prayers, he noticed another person praying in the darkened church. By the looks of the size of the man, it was probably Griz Sullivan. He walked up and sat in the pew in front of the man.

"Welcome, Griz. Nice to see you here. Do you live nearby?"

"Mr. Jorgen is putting me up for a while, until I can get on my feet."

Now that was a surprise. But Joseph felt proud of Mr. Jorgen's kindness. "He's a good man. A bit lonely since his wife passed, my wife tells me."

"I'm doing some odd jobs for him around the house, fixing the place up a bit. Not that I have much in the way of skills, but I'm strong and a quick learner. He doesn't like to admit it, but his back isn't what it used to be, and he's let some tasks go because of it."

"You're a praying man, I see." Joseph gestured toward the altar.

"I'm learning about that, too. You see, I did some things as a soldier that me and God are still working out."

"It's hard, sometimes," Joseph said, "being a man of faith and a soldier. Want to tell me about it?" It wasn't in Joseph's nature to reach out like this, but maybe a bit of Virginia was rubbing off on him. He figured she had introduced him to Griz for a reason and this must be it.

The big man took a deep breath. "Yeah, maybe I could talk about it here." He paused and looked around him. "Or maybe not. I wouldn't know where to start."

Joseph nodded and silently asked God to guide Griz's words and his own response. *Let me be your healing force for this man.*

Griz cleared his throat. "I enlisted as soon as I graduated from high school. I wanted to see the world and get away from the little town I grew up in. In Basic Training, I excelled at only one thing, and it wasn't long before I was seeing the world through the crosshairs of a rifle sight." The man growled low, like his namesake.

"I watched men die. Men I killed from a safe, hidden distance. I became unfeeling about it, until the very last time. That's when it all became very real. I watched my target step out on the balcony of his home. I squeezed the trigger. He fell, and while I still had him in my scope, a little boy ran up to his body and collapsed on top of it, crying. I couldn't hear him, but I know he was pleading with his daddy to get up."

Joseph rested his hand on Griz's shoulder, his own need for distance outweighed by the need to comfort.

"I couldn't go on after that. I fell apart. I sat there and cried as hard as that little boy did. I never knew my own daddy, and now I took one away from a little boy who did." The big man closed his eyes and hung his head. "I sit here now, asking God to forgive me, not just for that man, but all the others I murdered."

Joseph spoke with assurance. "He does forgive you. He

128

forgave you as soon as you were sorry. The hard part now is believing that, and forgiving yourself."

Chapter 9

On Sunday morning before Mass, Sam pulled Joseph aside. "I have to tell you about an idea Griz had."

"I should greet Father Kohler and help him get ready for his first Mass here," Joseph answered.

"I'll be quick," Sam said. "Griz took a look around him at the veteran gathering. He noticed how badly every building needs painting. I told him it's been cut out of the budget three years straight now and might be again. It's the only expense big enough that cutting it would cover the school's shortfall."

Joseph could see why it had been cut before. Though the church needed paint for good maintenance, the teachers needed their fair salaries even more. But the longer the building went without paint, the more it was becoming a matter of poor stewardship, rather than just aesthetics. Peeling paint left to the elements would mean rotting wood that would be much more expensive to replace.

"Griz says he and the younger vets will do the labor. Says it's the least they can do for a parish that supports them. I asked around, and I think the older vets will contribute some of the paint. For the rest, I plan on having a Sponsor-a-Gallon-of-Paint drive. For thirty bucks, I think enough parishioners would be happy to do their part. Then the unneeded paint budget can get the school through the final month of the year."

Joseph was delighted. He had not been able to find another option. "Sounds like your care for our vets has saved the day!"

"Maybe the day, but the problem remains. We don't bring in enough money to keep the school." With that the older man turned and entered the church. A paint chip fluttered to the ground as the door closed behind him.

When Father Mike Kohler finished his sermon during his first Mass at Guardian Angels, Private Ben Santini, the man Virginia had watched kick an imaginary suspended ball, raised a trumpet to his lips and began to blow a slow, perfectly pitched Taps. Sam Jorgen led several of the vets in a procession that accompanied the United States Flag to the alter. The congregation stood, some saluting while others covered their hearts with their hands. Virginia felt quite moved, and grateful for the liberty these soldiers and others like them had won for the country. When the last notes of Taps died out, the flag was retired to the rear of the church in complete silence, and Memorial Day had been honored.

Mass continued and after Father Mike's final blessing, he asked the parishioners to sit again and invited Virginia to the microphone. Joseph stood and let her out of the pew so she could go to the altar to speak. Virginia knew Joseph wasn't sure she was doing the right thing, but he told her to follow God's leading. She hoped she was right. Figuring out God's will was new to her. She had been raised to be honest, do what was right, and not hurt others, but discerning what God wanted beyond that was still confusing.

She scanned the congregation, recognizing several people she had shared time with over her kitchen table. Sam Jorgen and Griz Sullivan sat together. Her friend Heartie smiled encouragement. She and her mom would be moving soon. Virginia lowered the mic to her mouth. "Good morning, everyone. For those of you who don't know me, my name is Virginia and I'm Joseph's wife. But before I met him—"

She considered her wording. She had been a prostitute, but that term didn't tell the whole story.

"—I had been a victim of child trafficking for two years. Then, Joseph rescued me. He was ready to be ordained a deacon in preparation to be a priest, but God told him to marry me." She paused and looked at him with tenderness, once again amazed at the truth.

"He did."

She went on to talk about how she had been forced into prostitution and held against her will. How she had finally been trusted enough to be allowed on the street, though watched so carefully as to make escape nearly impossible.

"But nothing is impossible with God. Joseph says that all the time." She smiled at him. He nodded.

The congregation was silent and she could tell she had shocked them. One woman stood and left with her children. A man leaned back and crossed his arms, his judgment clear on his face. But she continued. She needed their help.

"I suspected that little boys were being held and used, or at least being groomed to the same occupation as me. It took a while, I'm ashamed to say, for me to find courage. You see, in the city where I worked, some of the police knew and looked the other way. It took time for me to learn to follow God's lead and to trust good would come out of it. So not long ago, I went to the local police and told my story in hope that maybe they could help the boys and the other women like me.

"You probably saw the story in the newspaper yesterday. Two days ago, our police arranged a raid, and the man who ran the operation was apprehended. They rescued five boys, some as young as nine." A soft audible gasp rose and Virginia gave the reaction time to settle. "As well as young women, ranging from 16 on up."

"I'm asking for your help. The boys will be returned to their families as soon as possible, as will the girls who have families—not all do—once they are ready. In the meantime, a convent has agreed to take them in and could use some help financing their necessities. But what these women need most is a new start. Some job training, inexpensive apartments, and friends. Please see me if you think you can help."

Joseph stood and came to her side. "I also have a request. Not all the criminals who ran this operation have been arrested. The media has published that the informant gave her statement to our local police. They may come here to retaliate, or to prevent Virginia and the other women from testifying. Please keep your eyes open and let the police know if you see anything suspicious.

"Now, let's have a round of applause for Father Kohler, who will start saying the 9:30 Sunday Mass weekly. And thanks to his parish for sharing him!"

Most of the congregation stood and applauded, and Virginia blushed, for it was clear they were expressing their support for her, too. She felt God blessing her.

It didn't stop there. Father Kohler invited her to come talk to his parish an hour later at his next Mass. She returned with generous donations to add to the money and business cards the people at Guardian Angels had pressed into her hand.

Joseph smiled at the triumphant look on Virginia's face as she came into his office after returning from Blessed Trinity. He felt proud of her and tender, too. And protective. He wished he were man enough to take her in his arms and hold her close.

"Joseph, are you terribly busy? Would you be able to drive me to the convent?"

"Right now?"

"Yes, I want to bring them the two parishes' donations. People were really generous, and I know the sisters will need some extra help to fill the needs of the girls for however long they are with them."

Joseph searched for an excuse. The last thing he wanted to do was surround himself with prostitutes. He finally had stopped thinking of Virginia that way, but this would bring it all up again, make her past harder to ignore.

"Do you really think we should visit them? Couldn't we mail the sisters a check? It could be there in a day or two."

Virginia sat in the chair near his desk, looking

disappointed. "I'd like to see the girls. I want to talk to them and know they're doing well. Maybe hear what they hope to do now. I don't want to abandon them to the unknown. And it would be fun to see the sisters again. They did so much for me when I needed it."

After a few moments of silence, Joseph looked back down at the Scripture he had been studying. Maybe it would help Virginia understand. He read aloud, "Finally, brothers and sisters, whatever is true, whatever is noble, whatever is right, whatever is pure, whatever is lovely, whatever is admirable—if anything is excellent or praiseworthy—think about such things. Philippians 4:8."

He glanced up at her to see if she understood that they should avoid the darker side of life. Instead he watched a tear spill out and roll down her cheek.

"You mean you don't want to go see them because they aren't pure? Is that how you saw me, too? Or maybe still see me?"

His gut tightened. This was not how he meant for this to go.

"Joseph, I admit I'm still further than most from being true and noble and pure, but nobody is all those things, so nobody would be left for you to think about. Is that what you suppose God wants?"

She wiped at the tear and sniffed. "You've had so much more instruction in these things, but I went to church as a girl, and I remember what my grandmother believed and what our preacher said. I think God wants us to look at each person and, rather than dwell on their obvious faults and mistakes, find what is true and noble and pure inside them and help them see it! We are supposed to find God in them, not stay away from them because they aren't perfect!"

She rose and hurried out of the room. He could hear her bedroom door close, followed by muffled crying.

He hated scenes. He hated that he had made her cry. And he really hated the realization that she was right. He remembered the story of the Good Samaritan, who stopped to help a man beaten by robbers after both a priest and a Levite had crossed the road to avoid the half-dead man.

He thought of Jesus, and his treatment of the untouchables of his time. The Lord healed the lepers, forgave the adulterers, and dined with tax collectors. To each of these he bestowed joy and faith.

Eyes lowered, Joseph noticed the verse before the one he'd read aloud. "And the peace of God, which transcends all understanding, will guard your hearts and your minds in Christ Jesus." He felt twice accused. He didn't want to visit those poor women in need because he didn't trust himself to keep his own thoughts pure, or remember what his wife had been. But here was God's word telling him that Jesus himself would guard his heart and mind.

He had the knowledge and training of a man of God, but needed sweet Virginia, with her gentle heart, to teach him about loving God's people. He picked up his car keys and prepared his sincere apology.

An hour later they parked in front of the convent. Before he'd even opened his door, Virginia had sprung from her seat and was ringing the doorbell. He chuckled. "Wait for me!"

She turned, her mood completely lifted, and blessed him with one of her wide-eyed, cheek-to-cheek grins. "Hurry up, then!"

He was at her side when Sister Angela opened the door and welcomed them inside. Virginia hugged her, an obvious pleasant surprise to the nun.

Virginia fanned her wad of money out for view, "Look what the parishes have sent to help out with the girls!"

"God is good," the little nun whispered.

"All the time!" Virginia answered and then asked to see Mother Margaret.

Sister Angela led them into a larger parlor than when Joseph had brought his family to introduce them to Virginia. Reverend Mother Margaret sat in the room in a circle of chairs among several girls and women who seemed a bit dazed. They must have just arrived since they all had their bags of belongings on their laps or at their feet. None wore much makeup, if any, and except for their tight, provocative clothing, this might have been a gathering of regular parish women. Joseph reprimanded himself for the images of them he'd preconceived.

Mother Margaret stood and welcomed Virginia into her arms amid surprised comments like, "Ginger! Hey girl!" and, "Oh my goodness, you're pregnant!"

His happy wife stepped back from the hug, pressed her stack of bills into Mother Margaret's hands, and nodded while she smoothed her blouse to emphasize her baby bump. Joseph hadn't really looked at it before. The sight made him smile and feel a bit sappy. Then all eyes turned to him and he cleared his throat and studied the Oriental rug.

Virginia tugged on his arm. "Everybody, this is Joseph, my husband."

The reaction to that declaration caused bedlam. Several of the girls squealed and they all huddled around Virginia who showed them her wedding ring and tried to answer a dozen different questions at the same time. He wished again he'd bought her a diamond.

Joseph looked to Mother Margaret, shrugged his shoulders and followed her gesture to come sit beside her. When things had calmed a bit, Virginia sat next to him and caught them up to date on what had happened to her since the last time they saw her, including having gone to the police.

One woman stood. She looked at Joseph. "I'm Bunny, but used to be Edith and might be again. We're still kind of in a state of shock about the changes that have happened since Friday morning when the cops stormed our building. But I think we all want to say thank you to the one guy who thought about more than just himself and whisked our Ginger away."

He felt himself blushing. Virginia was the hero here. Not him. He looked at his wife and Bunny/Edith also turned to her.

"And Ginger, I don't know how to thank you. I don't know what lies ahead. None of us do. But we know what we won't be doing, and we owe that to you." The others nodded, or murmured their thanks, and quite a few wiped away tears.

The women told them about the morning raid, being awakened out of sleep, and assuming they were headed to jail. "But the cops were nice to us. They let us pack a few things and then took us to the hospital to be checked. The police talked to us there and took our statements. We showed the doctors the scars or wounds from Blade—"

Joseph felt, more than heard his wife inhale and tense.

"Blade's still out there," she said.

After a silence, Bunny said, "You better be careful, girl. He'd never think to look for us here, but he has ways of finding people."

"Your phones!" Virginia went pale. "Joseph says they might lead him to you. Do you have your phones?"

"No, a detective took them." This from a tall woman of about 35. "Sounds like we were lucky."

Virginia nodded. "I forgot mine at Bessie's apartment, or he'd have found me long ago."

Mother Margaret stood, and Joseph imagined her standing up to the fear in the room. She held out the money Virginia had given her. "Look what Virginia brought from her parish! We'll start with getting you each some changes of clothes from the second-hand store, and add a few groceries to our larder. This afternoon I'd like to meet with you individually to see how we can help the most. We can get you in touch with relatives, buy some bus tickets, or maybe sign you up for trades classes, but I want you to know you are welcome to stay here and rest and renew for as long as you need to."

Sister Angela entered with a tea tray and a large bowl of cookies.

"Not everybody is here. Where are the others? Virginia asked.

Bunny nodded. "Some stayed at the hospital and will go to detox. Babs and Trudy slipped away before the rest of us noticed they weren't with us. I'm afraid they're probably back on the street already."

She frowned. "Ginger, did you know about the boys? The cops brought some boys out of the next building."

Virginia told them about the redheaded boy she had seen from the window and how he'd given her the courage to go to the police.

"Those dirt bags," said a bleached blonde.

"They were such little ones!" said a woman with browning teeth. "I'd have strangled Shank myself if I'd known."

Joseph marveled at the sympathy these women felt. And the fierce protectiveness. He was ashamed he had misjudged them.

Monday morning the clinic called and asked Virginia to come in to talk to her midwife, Manda. She exhaled slowly and tried to calm herself. Good news they would have given her over the phone. The gentle voice on the other end of the phone suggested she bring someone with her. Virginia considered that. She could walk next door to the church and ask Joseph to accompany her, and she knew he'd drop everything and come. But did she want him to?

She decided to protect him a while longer from the suspected new turn their lives would take. He had done enough. Maybe he didn't have to know yet. She could spare him some time worrying about her and their future. He had enough to deal with in this parish of wounded souls.

Putting on the best smile she could, she asked Claire if she could use her bicycle and started to pedal toward a diagnosis she wanted to avoid at all costs, but knew she couldn't. The receptionist showed her to the midwife's office.

Manda stood and her eyes shone with a sympathy that made Virginia wish she could protect herself from all it meant.

"Is it cancer?" She might as well face the truth as quickly as possible.

"Yes, I'm sorry. And it's an aggressive type. We need to start treatment right away."

They both sat, Virginia because her legs buckled. She took a moment and then decided with unshakeable conviction. She straightened her back. "I don't want to do anything until the baby is born."

"No, Virginia. We need to act now. We will remove the tumor and then begin—"

"No. The baby's safety needs to come first."

"You need to live so the baby can survive. You're in your second trimester. We can begin to treat you with minimal danger

138

to the baby. But if we don't, I can't guarantee you'll live long enough to bring it to full term."

It wasn't enough that Blade would be looking for her. Or that she had to deal with a shameful past. Or that she was alone in this world except for a rather odd man who had taken her in. But now cancer had forced her into a race to survive long enough to deliver this beloved child.

"How long do I have without treatment?"

"I can't say. This type of cancer metastasizes. Once it spreads to organs, you can deteriorate quickly. We should operate as soon as possible, and test lymph nodes to see if it's still contained."

"What's the danger to the baby if we do that?"

"I can't guarantee you the baby will be unharmed, but the odds are in its favor. We've come a long way in treatment strategies."

"Each week I give this child improves its chances, right?" Virginia asked.

"Yes, but I want to improve both your chances! Please, Virginia, trust me on this. Have the surgery soon."

She yearned to live and raise her little one. She imagined the weight of a little bundle in her arms and longing overtook her. But she'd never forgive herself if something went wrong and the baby didn't survive the operation. She listened to Manda about the risks and benefits of each option, but her baby would come first.

She needed time to think and to pray. Maybe God would tell her what to do, like he told Joseph to marry her. She doubted it, though. She didn't have quite the same relationship with God as Joseph did.

"I'll pray, Manda. And then I'll decide."

The midwife shook her head and the sympathy returned to her eyes. "Don't wait too long, Virginia."

As she pedaled towards home, Virginia passed the police station and her overwhelmed emotions jumped to another fear. She checked around her, half expecting, half terrified that she would see Blade's black sedan with the gold-trimmed wheels. If he didn't get her, the cancer would. Then a gentle sensation drew all her attention away from her worries. She stopped the bike. Another flutter stirred inside her. Her baby moved! She could feel the child and she would fight anyone and anything to protect it.

If she lived long enough to do so.

She felt her defensive wall rise against her emotions, but she shook her head. No, she wanted to feel every bit of this experience, even if proved excruciating to think about the separation from her child that death would bring. Tears streamed down her face as she began to peddle again. Even if this pregnancy only held the sadness of knowing she wouldn't live long, she would experience that sadness fully, while she fought to protect her child, giving him or her the best chance at a healthy birth.

Once at home, she parked, hurried upstairs to wash away evidence of crying, and approached Claire to thank her for letting her use the bicycle. Busy at her desk, Claire looked up from some work and her sweet smile made Virginia remember the goofy look on Joseph's face when he first met the parish secretary/youth minister/all-round assistant. Though Virginia had felt a little jealous of Claire when they met—the way she fit right in to parish life and seemed to be the kind of woman a minister would do well to marry—now she sincerely liked her.

She thought about her new diagnosis and braced herself against what the very real results might be. In only a few more months her husband might be trying to care for her baby without her. He would need help, and her child would need a mother.

Maybe if she and Joseph hadn't met, he'd have found Claire, or someone like her to marry. And with Claire's passion for those in need, she would be a great, nurturing mother.

"Claire, do you ever think of getting married?"

Claire tilted her head a bit and laughed. "Where did that come from?"

"You seem like you'd be a wonderful wife and mother. Surely there have been men who've thought so, too."

Claire looked around her and almost whispered. "What I am really hoping—and I haven't mentioned this to many people yet—I'm applying to convents. My dream is to be a nun!"

140

Virginia hoped her disappointment didn't show. Her plan for her baby's future fell apart as quickly as it had occurred to her. She shook herself loose from her thoughts.

"Claire, you'll make a wonderful sister. I stayed in a convent for a while and I can see how the life would be attractive. In fact, I think you should visit there. You'd love the women I knew."

"What's it named?" She picked up a pen and was ready to write.

"Mercy Convent. I'll get you their number." If she had known, she would have invited Claire to visit with them yesterday.

Virginia headed down the hallway to her kitchen. It had been an intriguing idea, but it didn't look like she'd be finding her own replacement.

Chapter 10

On Tuesday, Blade eased his Jaguar down the alley, out of view of the house that held the two people he slated for revenge. Only yesterday his DMV source had reported that the license registration of the car that took Gin had been updated. It all fit together. This was the town where the newspaper said the informant registered her story with the police.

And now he had found her. Ginger's john lived in the rectory of a church, and though he couldn't quite believe his own eyes, last night he had seen her walk with him in the front door like she owned the place. Like she wasn't a bimbo only a few weeks ago and a stool pigeon snitch now. He ached to hurt her, to make her pay for what she'd done, and his mind toyed with a long, slow retribution. But to really enjoy the process he needed to get her away from here. He'd find a place where he could take his time—and his pleasure—with her. With the star witness gone, maybe Shank would be released and they could start over somewhere fresh. Get past this sense of betrayal Blade felt when he thought of his brother.

He had the basics. Knife. Shovel. Duct tape, though he

probably wouldn't need it. He'd taught her not to scream a long time ago. The cop's handgun was in the glove box, but he hardly gave it a thought. They didn't call him Blade for nothing.

He slipped into the backyard of the rectory. Yes, there she was at the kitchen window washing dishes. He grinned. It was time.

Virginia relaxed with the warmth of her hands in the sudsy water and, as her mind wandered, she glanced out the window across the back yard of the rectory toward the alley. Two things happened at the same time, but seemed unconnected. The first was a white cloud of something that billowed between her and her alley-neighbor's yard. The second drove all curiosity about the cloud from her mind. Someone knocked hard on the kitchen door. She dried off her hands and headed to see who was there. She glanced down the hall towards Joseph's office first. Claire hadn't come in yet and Joseph had said he was going over to the church to do some cleaning. She wished she weren't alone.

She thought she had glimpsed Griz step back from her door and opened it with a smile. But then she froze.

"It's over, Gin. Come outside."

Blade!

"Outside!"

She obeyed automatically. The proper response had been knifed into her soon after she was "recruited."

Movement outside the sacristy window caught Joseph's eye. Strange. What could make a white cloud rise in the alley? He moved closer to the window and could see a black sedan parked just beyond the rectory yard. It seemed familiar. Then he remembered the Jaguar that parked while he first met his wife. And the driver who had threatened Virginia and prompted Joseph's decision to drive her away.

As he set down the sanitizing spray bottle, he saw Virginia step out of the back door and seem to walk willingly with that man! Why would she go with him? Why didn't she fight? Did she really want to go back to that life? She wouldn't if he could help it!

He ran to the side door, the unfinished scrubbing unnerving him, but not nearly as much as his concern for Virginia.

Blade gripped her arm like the jaws of a bear trap. "That's right, we don't want anything to happen to the reverend now, do we? You behave and maybe I won't give him what's coming to him. Though I wouldn't mind bringing his cute little sister into the business."

Please, God! No! Don't let him get his filthy hands on Meg!

The thought wrenched Virginia out of her blind obedience. She stomped on Blade's foot and tried to elbow him but Blade in one motion slid his grip down to her wrist, wrenched it behind her back, and lifted her almost off her feet. She screamed as he dragged her towards the alley. She refused to go easily, and twisted to get away. He jerked her wrist higher and the pain made her go limp. His other arm, which quickly found her windpipe and blocked her breathing, now wielded the knife that gave the monster his name.

How could she have forgotten so quickly the lessons he'd taught her? Lessons learned to the accompaniment of her pain and his grin. Never fight back. Don't make a sound. Never let him see your fear.

"You turned on Shank, Gin. It's one thing to disappear, but no one rats on Shank and lives if I can help it."

She wouldn't have pleaded with him even if she could speak. She had learned long ago how much he enjoyed that, and how useless it was. He tightened his hold as they moved toward the alley and she wondered if she'd still be conscious by the time they got there. If she blacked out she may never wake up again.

As Joseph burst out of the side of the church, he saw Virginia was no longer walking as if she had chosen to go. Blade was dragging her, his arm around her throat!

Fear gave way to action. Joseph flew across the lawn while his mind flashed him back to a war-torn desert village. The servant of God became a soldier again, hell-bent on protecting the innocent. This time the innocent wasn't a stranger, but his Virginia. His Gomer. A young woman who'd been forced into a life she didn't choose or want.

No one would force her back as long as he was alive.

The huge man saw him barreling toward them, and Joseph noticed something flash in his right hand. Good, it was a switchblade, not a gun. *Blade*, Joseph reminded himself. Now he understood the name. Unarmed himself, the odds weren't in Joseph's favor, though. Blade extended his knife toward Joseph and drew Virginia in front of him with his left arm, holding her close.

"Joseph, no!" Virginia screamed, but Blade slid his arm back up and cut off the air in her windpipe.

Joseph didn't slow. With all his momentum, he closed the distance between him and his enemy. He pivoted his full weight on his left foot. He kicked his right foot up and out, slammed it into the wrist that held the knife, heard a satisfying snap, and watched the switchblade fly out of reach. Before his foot touched back down, he grabbed the offending arm and twisted it. The force of Joseph's spin revolved the man away from Virginia and broke his grip.

Blade swore, clutching his arm close to his chest with his free hand. He looked for the knife, but Virginia had snatched it off the ground and backed out of reach while aiming it at his heart. She gulped deep breaths and then rasped, "I'm done with Shank. Done forever. You can tell him that a minister and a girl bested the fearsome Blade, or you can tell him I'm dead. I'd recommend the latter."

Blade looked at Joseph, perhaps gauging if he still had a chance, but whatever he saw in Joseph's face made him back towards his car while shouting, "You're worse than dead if you testify, Gin."

As Blade disappeared into the alley, Virginia crumpled to the ground.

Joseph ran to her and dropped to his knees in front of her. She crouched, trembling, all bravado gone. Joseph could feel his own adrenaline coursing through his veins and initiating a full-body shake. Too fired up to speak, he held and rocked Virginia hoping they could both calm down. His soul shot a heartfelt *thank you* to God and to one Sergeant Kick Box Kao.

He heard Blade's movements, but focused now on Virginia, all thought of any immediate danger from Blade pushed aside in his concern for his bride. He had heard the bone snap. It would be weeks before Blade could wield his knife again. Sounds barely registered: a shouted oath, a car door opening, Blade's body as he dropped into the seat, his rustling to get settled, the ignition turning the motor, windshield wipers, gears shifting into a roll—

Then he heard a trigger cocked and realized he should never have turned his back on his enemy.

Chapter 11

In a split millisecond, he was back on the battle field, and this time it wasn't Rusty who shielded him from incoming fire, but he who twisted to position himself between the Jaguar that backed up into view and Virginia, drawing her against his chest and shielding her. And in that same micro moment he understood. He finally realized the instinct that had flung Rusty between him and the gunfire and that now mobilized Joseph into the trajectory of danger. It was more than courage or selflessness; it was a deep, inborn, all-consuming need to protect that which was dear to him. For Rusty in that moment of war it had been his buddy Joe, his comrade-in-arms.

For Joseph, it was Virginia, a young woman who had already suffered more than anyone could understand at the hands of evil, and despite her abuse, still loved the good in the world enough to find it in him and connect her future to his. He shielded her because she was the most important part of himself, and it was more imperative to defend and protect her than to live.

He heard the shot at the same instant that he felt its force explode into his back and burn his gut. He heard and felt another shot hit his left upper arm, and then with relief heard the car shift and speed away. He couldn't support himself. Falling, he grabbed for Virginia, needing to know as he sank into the pain that he had succeeded. That she was safe. That the baby would survive.

She had gone limp. Scarlet blood spread across her white blouse.

He applied pressure to her chest with his palm. Though the sirens he heard should have raised hope, failure consumed him. The same deep shame of his last day in battle returned. He had carried the bleeding Rusty on his back to the truck, but he hadn't been able to save the man who had shielded him from death. And now he had failed to protect his wife and their child.

The lift onto a gurney was painful, but nowhere near as excruciating as knowing Virginia lay bleeding on a gurney next to him. He reached and grasped her hand, hoping for a squeeze or any movement to let him know she was going to make it. The paramedics worked on both of them, but seemed to know how important it was to let him keep hold of her hand as long as he could. How he wished he had taken every opportunity to do this in the weeks he'd known her. Tears of shame welled in his eyes. He should have held her, shown her how much he had grown in his love for her.

He lost sight of Virginia as they lifted her into her ambulance, but he could still feel the impression of the warmth of her hand in his. As he raised his bloodied hand and looked at it, a realization dawned slowly that yesterday would have given him joy. Today it seemed insignificant.

His worry about germs had vanished.

The odors of medicine in his ambulance didn't bother him. Exposure to disease held no threat. He looked around him at the monitors and equipment. Everything here was intended to help and heal. Yet, he no longer cared about himself. If there were any way, he would trade his health for his wife's.

God, please save Virginia. Don't let her die! I want to spend a lifetime loving her the way I should have.

He focused on the memory of his last view of her face. She looked so pale! His attention shifted as an EMT came into focus.

"He's lost a lot of blood," one paramedic said to the other.

Joseph recognized the truth of his words. Weakness enveloped him, and the pain in his back and arm increased as he turned his thoughts to his wounds. Yet he also knew with deep conviction that he would never again be plagued by germ phobia. And he knew the moment it stopped. He heard again the crack of Blade's bone when he drove his foot into his arm. He felt his pulse quicken at the thought, and then his heart monitor set off an alarm.

"Please," he begged the EMT with the last of his breath, "do all you can to save my wife and child." Then pain beyond any he had known before, even at war, clenched his chest, and he heard the EMT shout, "Cardiac arrest!"

Chapter 12

Virginia woke to pain, confusion, and a bustling nurse.
She was surrounded by curtains and the room was too bright.
"You're in ICU. You had a bullet lodged in your breast
and they removed it."

Removed the bullet? The breast? The memory of Blade's
attack returned and she gasped, "Joseph? Is he alive!?!" A
beeping increased in speed and she turned to look behind her
toward the sound. But movement shot pain across her chest and
dropped her head back to the pillow. She pled silently with her
eyes.

"I know they brought him in with you, but I don't know
his condition. The doctor will come in soon to talk to you. You
are one lucky lady, they say. The bullet lodged near a tumor.
They took that out, too." The nurse moved out of Virginia's view
and she heard soft footsteps become fainter.

Lucky?

She didn't know if the baby was safe! "Nurse!" The effort
of the call brought a new spasm of pain.

The footsteps approached. "You need to try to stay calm.

150

You've been through a lot."

"I'm pregnant." *Am I still pregnant?*

"Yes, shhh now. Calm down. Your husband told the ambulance crew. Baby's heart rate is fine. It's better than yours at the moment. You need to try to quiet yourself, for both your sakes. How's your pain level?"

Pain? Yes, she hurt, but what did that matter compared to knowing her sweet baby lived? If only she knew the same about her husband. "I'm OK. Please find out about Joseph."

"I'll tell you as soon as I know anything."

The nurse adjusted something above her, and Virginia slipped back into blessed sleep.

Joseph floated weightless. Bodiless. Deeply, deeply calm. He didn't really look around him, but became aware of, what? Light? Colors? Neither of those words were accurate. If he combined warmth and beauty and joy, those sensations together might be close to what he was experiencing. There was a flow, too, a directional wave moving toward him and pulsing. Or was it harmonizing with the heat and the loveliness and the pleasure? The wave's color—if you could call it that—changed, and he sensed it emanated from Virginia and flowed toward him. Was this the grace of prayer? Or love? Yes, he felt her love for him and it lifted him, surrounding him with support. He basked in it and then his love for Virginia rose and the flow became bidirectional. He hoped it embraced her as it did him.

The current changed again, all ripples and rainbows. A rich royal purple dominated the other colors and he knew his mother was sending this emanation. He couldn't see her but he was aware of her worry and her prayer for his strength. Another light flowed alongside his mother's and wafted a scent as delicious as any flower he'd ever smelled. His sister Meg was loving him. Though he was unaware of any body sensations, he swelled within himself. His heart reached toward them. Not the blood pumping heart, but the center of himself. His soul. Yes, his soul was communicating with the souls of his loved ones. And that merging of care, that melting and flowing and pulsing and harmonic music, touched him with God's infinite love and beckoned him into something purer and deeper.

He envisioned his loved ones and could see his mother and Meg boarding an airplane. He knew the prayers that were in their hearts as surely as the rosary beads that were in his mother's grasp. He next glimpsed Virginia on an operating table. He raised his thoughts and trusted the Love that surrounded him. *Lord, be with her. Heal her. Let her know you.*

The surgical scene was replaced with a dining room. Virginia was at the table, laughing at something his sister had said. She leaned back and he could see a child in a highchair beyond her. Their child. A healthy and happy, pink-faced little girl. She mashed a cupcake into her mouth and her eyes widened with the delight of her first taste of frosting. The room reverberated with joy and filled him instantly with the same. His mother carried a bowl of steaming spaghetti into the room and laughed. "She couldn't wait until dessert for her birthday cupcake?"

They were all safe. Even though he wasn't there, they were together and able to laugh. His wife and daughter had found a place in his loving family. Was this a moment of decision? Was the Love that surrounded him offering him a choice? Gratitude surged for the gift of knowing his family would reach a place of happiness. He could go on to contribute to the flowing harmony and be part of the infinite praise and joy.

Virginia awoke in the morning to a light knock on her hospital door. She had been moved during the night to a regular room, so much quieter than the bustle and beeps of the ICU. A pleasant looking, blonde-haired young woman in jeans peeked in. "Are you feeling well enough for visitors? I have a young man here who insists on seeing you."

Virginia gave a weak smile and a nod, hoping it was her husband. She hadn't heard anything about Joseph yet and longed to see him safe with her own eyes.

Then in tip-toed the redheaded boy whose terrified face had haunted her into talking to the police. He was alive, and free, and smiling!

"Wonderful boy!" She forced more words out. "So glad to

see you! I was scared when the police said they didn't find you." She heard a bit of slur to her speech and didn't know if it was from weakness or pain medicine.

He grinned and handed her a crayon drawing but, not speaking, looked to his mother.

"This is Ryan, and I'm Maeve. And he and I are so very, very grateful to you." The mother's eyes brimmed and she wiped them quickly. "I was terrified I'd never see him again when he disappeared. We still aren't quite sure how it all happened, but Ryan showed up at my door the same night as the police raid."

Virginia looked at the drawing, partly to give the mother time to collect herself. Holding back the black scribbled night, a yellow window frame took up most of the paper. A face with red crayon curls looked down from it. At the bottom of the page he had carefully printed, "I knew you'd help."

She wished she could hug him, but moving still brought pain. She reached out and he placed his hand in hers. She gave it a little squeeze. "I'm very, very sorry it took a long time." Her own eyes filled and tears warmed trails down her cheeks. "I was scared. But I knew you were, too. I wish I had helped faster."

With a glance at the mother, Virginia asked wordlessly if Ryan was doing all right.

"Ryan's glad to be back home. He hasn't quite found his voice yet, though. He hasn't talked to anyone since that night."

The words broke Virginia's heart, and her own voice momentarily failed her.

"We'd better go. We don't want to tire you, and we have a long drive home. But Ryan heard about you being shot on the news and he wouldn't calm down until I told him we would try to see you, or at least leave you his drawing."

The mother said their goodbyes and they slipped out of the room.

Moments later, Virginia heard running steps in the hallway. Ryan's head peeked into her room. He took a deep breath and blurted, "S-sorry you're hurt. Th-thanks for saving us." Then, as quickly, he was gone.

Even with the pain that each breath brought to her chest, Virginia knew she'd choose the same path to the police again in a heartbeat. And yet, she'd caused Joseph to be shot by that decision. She turned her thoughts to him and desperate prayers to God for his wellbeing.

Again, Virginia awoke to a tapping on her door. "Come in," she rasped. She felt stronger than the last time she woke.

Mr. Jorgen and Detective Kate entered together.

"I wanted my two heroes to have a little time together," Kate said, "but the nurse made us promise no more than five minutes."

"Two heroes?" Talking was an exertion. She hoped they'd do most of it.

"You," Kate said, "and Mr. Jorgen, who called 911 and got ambulances to you in time."

Mr. Jorgen's face was ashen. "Or maybe I'm the guy who caused you to get shot. I never would have done what I did if I had known it would put you and Joseph in the hospital. The nurses couldn't tell us about him. I think he's still in ICU."

Kate settled in the chair next to the bed. "That wasn't your fault, Mr. Jorgen, believe me. But tell her what you mean."

"I'd been on my way to the rectory with a ten-pound bag of flour, the bag my wife had asked me to go buy the day she died from a brain embolism." He sighed. "The flour that meant I wasn't with her when she passed away so sudden. Well, I hated that bag of flour and figured you could use it, what with all the baking you do. I was carrying it over to you when I saw that sneaky perp park his fancy Jaguar in the alley and then go up to the back door of the rectory. I was afraid he was going to kidnap you and take you back."

"Mr. Jorgen did some serious quick thinking." Kate urged him to go on.

"Between my fear for you and my anger at that bag of flour, I jabbed it open and then threw it against his windshield. It was a good direct hit and would completely block his view. I called 911 when I saw the knife in his hand and Joseph running toward him. After telling them what was happening, I tossed my phone under his seat so he could be traced if he did get you into the car and drive away. But when he got to the car—I was hiding but watching—he saw the windshield, let out a curse, got in and backed up, and then pulled the handgun out from somewhere. I keep thinking if he could have driven off he might not have shot you." At the last few words Mr. Jorgen's voice broke, and he pulled out a large handkerchief to blow his nose.

"Blade wasn't going to let me live to testify, Mr. Jorgen. He would have taken me somewhere isolated to kill me," *slowly*, she thought but didn't say. "You saved my life," she assured him. She looked at Kate. "Is he in custody?"

"He took off before the police and ambulances arrived, but Mr. Jorgen's phone did the trick. He only made it a few miles away before he was surrounded. We took him to a different hospital to have his broken arm set. Not taking any chances." Kate's voice changed. "He's at the jail now, safely behind bars. When I left there, some priest was asking to talk to him.

Virginia shivered involuntarily. Even she had underestimated how frightened she had continued to be of Blade, after Joseph had taken her away from him. For the first time in more than two years, she felt like she could set that fear aside.

But why would no one tell her about Joseph? She reassured herself that Mr. Jorgen thought he was in ICU. That should mean he was still alive.

Low chimes swelled into rich notes of a cello. Then Joseph became aware of an aroma. Something wafted toward him, incensed with sandalwood and the copper brown color of a madrone tree trunk. A familiar priest was standing before him.

"Father Mike! Is this heaven? Are you here, too?" The questions voiced no distress, for the joy that flowed and harmonized around him prevented fear.

"I'm with you in my prayers. I've been where you are. I don't know if it's heaven. I think of it more as a decision place. I visited it as a child, when I was dying of cancer. Back then I called it being in a rainbow, but now I refer to it as the River of Glory."

"But you left?" The idea seemed hard to believe. Would anyone choose to leave this experience of delight... not to the senses exactly... maybe to the soul? "God is here." It wasn't a question but an acknowledgement, and Joseph again swelled with gratitude for the Love he now knew.

"I doubt everyone gets a choice. I don't know why I did, but I couldn't stay in such bliss, knowing my parents needed me and the pain that it would bring them. Yet part of the experience never left me. When I pray and truly center, I can still join in the River and know the Love and joy again."

Father Mike turned around and gestured. Suddenly the fullness of a symphony, the shattering of light into a prism of colors, and multiple aromas of nature surged toward Joseph. They emanated from his congregation, with a particularly vibrant flow from his new veteran friends. He could see them now. They were gathered at Guardian Angels Church, led in prayer by Father Mike. Their love so enveloped him that his body proved too limited to endure it.

He could give himself up to the Love, or bear some separation for the time being, for the sake of others. Before something burst he needed to choose, and he did, but as the cataclysm subsided, he was embraced by the blue and silver smell of a uniform, the sense of being wrapped as a child into a fierce bear hug, and the unmistakable laughter of his dad. Beyond his father—within a blend of old country ballads, wafted ribbons of the smells of roast beef, machine oil, dairy cows, and soap—emanated reminders of his grandparents.

"See you after my shift!" Joseph said, as his dad used to call to him every time he left for work.

When Virginia opened her eyes the next time, a white-jacketed woman was making notes on a clipboard.

"Nurse? My husband?"

"Well, hello there! Welcome to the land of the living! I'm Dr. Lee, I was your surgeon. We are calling you Miracle Lady."

"Please, how is Joseph? Is he alive?"

"I'm sorry, of course that's what you want to know first. His surgeon came by once earlier to talk to you but you were asleep."

Virginia didn't know if she could stand one more delay. Where was Joseph? How was he? *Dear Grandma's God, let him*

156

be safe!

"It was touch and go for a while, I'm told. His surgery took hours and we nearly lost him, but he is out of immediate danger. One of the bullets did serious damage to his spine and a kidney. The other passed through his arm and found its way to your breast tumor. Sounds to me like he saved your life twice over. Quite a husband you have there, Mrs. O'Keefe."

"Three times now."

"I'm sorry?"

"He's saved me three times." However, the relief that washed over her brought such a release of tears that she couldn't say more. She turned instead to silent prayer. *Thank you, thank you, God. You have been so good to me, beyond anything I ever deserved. Thank you for sparing his life. Thank you that the baby is still safe.*

"You really were lucky, or blessed. I just talked to your midwife and heard you had been refusing surgery. The tumor hadn't spread when we took it, but it was a very malignant type and you probably wouldn't have survived long enough to bring your little one into the world. But your husband had told the EMTs to do anything necessary to keep you and your baby alive. His words inspired me and the surgery team. We wanted to do whatever we could so he could hold you both when the time comes."

Virginia thanked the doctor, who finished a quick check of her sutures and hurried on her way. Virginia's thoughts turned back to God. *Thank you that you turned such evil into a way to heal me when I wouldn't have let the doctors operate if I'd been conscious. Horrible things have happened, but I can see now you were with me through every minute of it. I think you suffered right along with me, though I was here-and-now and you were on the cross long ago.*

I don't know how serious Joseph's wounds are but I promise you, I will take care of him the rest of my life and love him for all that time, too.

Virginia felt a flutter of movement near her belly button and her prayers of thanks became a surge of praise. She loved this child, her husband, and their God.

Chapter 13

Joseph first became aware of the smell of antiseptic. Then of the beeps of his monitors.

Hospital.

But he also recognized a change in himself. He was without fear or anxiety. He felt secure and cared for deeply. God was with him. Not the experience of God he'd had before: the leader, director, the commander of his life. Rather, this awareness of God was more brother and friend and beloved. He rested in the experience and smiled.

"He smiled!" It was his mother's voice. "I'm sure he did. Joseph? Are you awake?" He wanted to smooth the worry out of her voice. He was loved. His family members were loved. All would be well.

He opened his eyes and took in the white blanket that covered him, the bed rails, the dry erase board on the wall, and his mother in the chair next to his bed, leaning close.

"Mom. I'm good."

"Oh, thank God. We were afraid we were going to lose you." She sat back and regained her normal composure, but her eyes were a bit swollen and she looked so very weary.

He knew Virginia was OK, though he didn't quite remember how he knew that, so he asked, "Virginia?"

"She's going to be fine, Joseph. They are saying you were quite the hero. You protected her... and my grandchild, I might add." His mother went on to tell him about the tumor and how the bullet had directed the surgeon's attention to it. He hadn't known about that.

"Cancer?"

"A particularly malignant type, though it hadn't metastasized."

He sobered at the thought of what might have happened to Virginia and the baby, yet that thought enriched the sense of trust he had experienced since he awoke.

His sister moved into view on the other side of the bed. "Hey, JoJo, good to see you alive." She looked as weary as his mother. "I'm going to go see Virginia now that I know you are awake. She's been a bit frantic for news about you." She kissed his cheek and headed toward the door.

"Meg?" he said.

"Yes?"

"Tell her I love her." He would do that himself as soon as he could and on every day God gave them after that.

Father Mike entered the room as she left. Joseph introduced him but the words seemed such an effort. "Mom, Father Mike. New friend." He had a glimpse of Father Mike within a rainbow and he felt he'd seen the image somewhere before. Probably a dream.

The priest shook her hand, and momentarily rested his other hand on her shoulder. "Nice to meet you, Mrs. O'Keefe. How are you holding up? I'm sure the last couple of days have been rough."

Joseph watched his mother size up Father Mike and then nod. She had decided she liked him.

"Wait, couple of days?"

"It's Thursday, Dear. You were shot on Tuesday morning. Meg and I came Tuesday night.

"Both at my bedside since then, right? Mom, I'm going to

be OK. Go get some rest."

"I saw the doctor in the hallway," said Father Mike. "He is coming to talk to you. Maybe your mother would like to hear what he says before she rests."

Joseph took a deep breath to help his words flow. "That's why you're here? Doctor asked you to come?" It must be bad news if the doctor thought he needed a spiritual friend at his side.

"He did, when he saw me in the hall, but I was on my way to visit you anyway."

The doctor knocked softly on the door and entered.

Joseph tried to sit up to greet him. That was the first that he began to realize the extent of his injuries. His left arm wouldn't bear his weight. He looked at the bandage from his elbow to his shoulder. He shifted to his other side expecting that arm to help him sit up, but the pain from the effort dissuaded him. His abdomen felt like Blade's knife had found its target. He tried to draw up his knees to ease the hurt but nothing happened. His legs. He couldn't feel his legs at all.

He looked to the doctor.

"I'm Doctor Velasco, your surgeon. It's best to lie still until you've done a little more healing. We'll have the physical therapist in to begin work with you in another day or two.

"One bullet pierced your arm with a clean entry and exit wound."

And settled in Virginia's chest, Joseph realized and cringed. He focused back on the surgeon.

"Only muscle damage as far as we can tell. Missed your bone and major nerves and the artery. The other wasn't quite so easy. It seriously damaged your spinal cord and a couple vertebrae, as well as your right kidney. I'm afraid we had to remove the organ."

"I can't feel my legs. But I feel back and gut pain."

The doctor waited. He knew what Joseph needed to ask.

Joseph straightened himself as well as he could, facing the question at attention. "Will I walk?"

His mother covered her mouth, but he could see the misery in her eyes.

The doctor's shoulders drooped. "No, Joseph. Not this

160

side of heaven. But I want you to know you will always stand tall as a hero to many."

Joseph allowed himself a slow inhale and exhale, then drew on the strength that he attributed as a gift from God, and from the people who had been praying for him. "If it's God's will to heal me, he will. But until then I know some vets who can lead me down the path ahead."

Father Mike squeezed Joseph's good shoulder and nodded.

His mother cleared her throat, sniffed, and blinked back tears. "And I know three women who will be there for whatever you need."

Three. Yes. Virginia. It hardly seemed fair to saddle a brand-new wife with a husband experiencing mobility-impairment, but he knew she wasn't the type to abandon anyone in need.

He wouldn't be walking anytime soon, but the thought of Virginia brought a new question to mind. What else would he be unable to do? Perhaps this was God's answer to his promise of chastity and abstinence that he had intended to make when he was ordained. He would have more to ask his doctor or therapist about, but not now with a priest and his mother in the room.

As Dr. Velasco prepared to leave, he said, "I'll be back tomorrow and we'll talk more after you've had time to process."

"Doctor," Joseph said, extending his good hand, "thank you for using your skills. I know you did everything... the best outcome you could."

At this the man in the white coat met his gaze, shook hands, then nodded, clearly moved. A few minutes later, the doctor returned, pushing Virginia in a wheelchair and followed by Meg.

His wife! Joseph wanted to rush to her side and swirl her around the room. Instead he could only reach out his hand toward her. She grasped it and held it to her cheek. She couldn't stay long since he was still in ICU and, as far as he knew, this was probably her first effort at staying upright since her own surgery, but they had both needed to see each other.

"You're safe? Our baby's safe?" He knew it, but he had to

see her and hear it, too.

"We are, thanks to you. And Blade and Shank are behind bars. I'm not afraid anymore." Her bright face reinforced her words.

"Me neither." He squeezed her hand. "Not of germs. Not of our future."

Joseph's next visitor was Griz. He extended his hand to the new friend, who gave it a hearty shake.

"You tired of people asking how you're feeling yet?"

The man's white teeth were so striking against his dark skin that Joseph realized he must not have seen him smile before, or he would have remembered.

"Something tells me *you* are feeling better, am I right?" Joseph asked.

"I guess you are. I've done a lot of praying, what with you and Miz Virginia in danger. And I came to realize that I'm blessed. And I'm going to build something good of my life, not to make up for what I've done, because I can't bring back the people I've shot, but because God was good enough to forgive me, so the least I can do is accept that and forgive myself."

"Well said." Joseph realized he wasn't the only one with a new relationship with God.

"And I've talked to Father Mike. He said you're going to require some help with rehab, or therapy, or whatever you want to call it. He says the bishop will hire me to be your aide for as long as you need, assuming you agree."

"Do you suppose that means the bishop intends to keep me on, as well?" Joseph hadn't really worried about his job yet. Nothing seemed important enough to worry him, but the offer was welcome. "I would truly appreciate your help, Griz."

"I've been to visit Miz Virginia and told her about the plan. She's good with it, too, she says. But she wants to change my name." He looked chagrinned.

"Back to Eugene?"

"No, sir. She wants to call me Panda. She says Griz sounds too mean for a guy like me."

Joseph couldn't tell if the man was proud or embarrassed.

"Well, what do you want to be called?"

The white teeth shone again. "Just call me in time for her dinner rolls!"

The next day Meg rolled Virginia's wheelchair back into the Joseph's ICU cubicle, then discreetly announced she needed a soda. Her mother looked from Joseph to Virginia and decided it was a fine time to join her daughter.

The husband and wife held hands. "This is nice," said Virginia.

"I'm sorry we didn't do this before," Joseph answered.

"You're not worried about germs anymore?"

"Nope, that broke the same instant Blade's arm did, and though I'm not sure why, I'm not going to question it."

His wife met his gaze and held it. He fought back an emotional surge by clearing his throat. "Virginia, I've been awake enough to do some thinking." His dream about the vine had come back to him and he'd been analyzing it.

She tilted her head and waited.

"All along I've been figuring God sent me to rescue you."

"And now you don't?"

"I do, but I also realize he was giving me what I needed for my own rescue. You. You've broken through my fears and saved me from a self-centered pursuit of holiness. I realize now that we don't grow spiritually in a vacuum. We need other people to help and be helped as we struggle together to do God's will."

"You're saying I rescued you by putting you into a situation where you were shot, almost died," she lowered both her chin and her voice, "and might not walk again?"

He let go of her hand and lifted her chin with his good hand, the other arm lying bandaged across his chest. "You taught me how to love others, and that's one of the most important ways to show our love for God. Without being able to do that, we're like..." He struggled for how to express what he wanted to say, then remembering a verse from Corinthians, he smiled and recited:

"If I speak in the tongues of men or of angels, but do not have love, I am only a resounding gong or a clanging cymbal. If I

have the gift of prophecy and can fathom all mysteries and all knowledge, and if I have a faith that can move mountains, but do not have love, I am nothing. If I give all I possess to the poor and give over my body to hardship that I may boast, but do not have love, I gain nothing... And now these three remain: faith, hope and love. But the greatest of these is love."

"Virginia, I had faith, but you taught me love."

"And you gave me hope! Oh, Joseph, I was so scared when I didn't know if you were alive, and it seemed to take forever for someone to tell me you were. I realized then how, even though we were strangers married under the strangest of circumstances, I have come to love you dearly."

She leaned from her wheelchair and Joseph elbowed up to meet her for the first of what he hoped would be many, many kisses.

Blade sat in his cell, brooding and angry. His arm was killing him and so was being alone with his thoughts. He considered the cast ruefully. Too bad he hadn't started out with the gun, rather than his knife. He could have shot Gin and that john right in the head. His blade hadn't ever failed him so badly before. He never saw that kick coming, and he still didn't know how that preacher pulled off the maneuver that broke his wrist and his hold on Gin. He thought it through for the thousandth time. One minute his arm exploded in pain and then next the guy's foot was in his face.

How many days had he sat in this cell? Was it three? After the cops had surrounded him, they took him to the hospital. Guarded him close or he might have tried to run for it once the cast was on. Might have gone back to Gin and finished the job. But no, they'd brought him to this hell hole. He looked around the four graffitied walls that smelled of sweat and urine. How could he spend another day sitting here, alone with his thoughts?

If only he was at least in the same jail as Shank, but he and the guys were a couple hundred miles away. The thought of his brother brought no comfort. He'd failed Shank. That look had told him to take care of the informer and he hadn't. But his brother had failed him, too. He relived sitting in his car the night they led the little boys out of the building next to the house. Shank had lied to him, outright. Kidnap scheme he'd said. Trust me, he'd said.

He wanted to pound somebody. He would have pounded the wall, but he'd tried that yesterday when his anger got the better of him. All that had done was send excruciating pain up his good arm. Better yet, he wanted to cut somebody. Cutting had always relieved him of emotion. If only he still had his knife. Last time he saw it, it was in Gin's hand and she had the nerve to point it at him! Him! Blade! His own knife.

The guard approached his cell. "That priest is back. You want to see him today?"

Why not? He'd turned him away every day he'd been here. The guy obviously wasn't going to give up. At least he wouldn't be alone for a while. "Yeah, sure."

Footsteps neared. He'd hoped he might have been taken out of the cell, but no. No escape.

The priest pulled up a chair and sat outside his bars. Beyond his reach.

"I'm Father Mike Kohler. I thought you might like someone to talk to."

"And say what? 'Please, Father, hear my confession?' Yeah, right. I'm no Catholic."

"Say whatever you want to say. I'm just here to visit."

"Well, I'm just here to sit. To rot, I suppose." He changed tactics. "I'm innocent, you know. They got the wrong guy."

Father What's-his-name didn't seem convinced. "We're all innocent of some things and guilty of others."

Blade tried another angle. "You know, I'm the guy who brought the red-headed kid home." There, he'd caught the priest's interest. Watched him sit a bit forward in his chair. Not within reach still, but certainly intrigued.

"Ryan, that was his name. I found him wandering out on the street. Seemed a bit dopey, like drugged maybe. I asked him where he lived and drove him home, took him to the suburbs."

"That was a great thing to do, Blade. The police hadn't figured out how that happened. You made the boy and his mom truly happy with that decision."

The image of that doorway hug came back to mind. He nodded. It was a good thing to do and made him feel almost good about himself. That didn't last long.

So, the kid hadn't talked yet. Hadn't told them he was also the one who snatched him and brought him to his brother like a lamb to be butchered. "Yeah, well, I didn't want nothing bad to happen to the kid. Little kids should be safe." He swore under his breath.

"Did something happen to you when you were a kid, Blade?" The priest's words were soft. This guy was smooth. He'd better watch himself or he'd be sniveling about his mom and her devil of a boyfriend. They'd pin a murder on him, and he'd never get out of this place. He'd say no more. But why did this guy have to bring all that back to mind? He turned his back to the bars.

The priest waited a few more minutes, then stood. "I'll be back, Blade. We can talk some more when you're ready. I want to leave you with something to think about, though. There's nothing God won't forgive, if we're sorry."

Father Bud Morris knocked at Joseph's door and entered.

"Thank God you're alive to visit," he said. "I'm sorry about what happened. It sounded more like a movie than real life. No, don't trouble yourself."

Joseph had tried to sit more upright. Now that he was out of ICU, a bar was suspended above him to help him adjust his position in bed. Soon, they said, it would help him get out of bed, though with only one good arm, even a slight pull on it wore him out.

"It's really nice of you to come visit." For the first time without a qualm, Joseph offered his hand to his mentor.

"What, no sanitizer?"

"Believe it or not, those days are gone."

The priest shook hands with him, then drew a chair near the bed and sat. "What was the breakthrough? It seems a small miracle."

"I'm afraid the breakthrough was breaking someone's wrist, and I don't feel properly repentant yet, either. I think it had something to do with taking control of a situation, rather than being a victim of fear."

"I'm delighted to hear it. I thought you were born with some OCD thing that was here to stay."

"Actually, it only started the first time I was shot. Seems like a weird kind of justice that it should end the second time I was shot."

Father Morris retrieved his pipe from his pocket, but when Joseph lifted his eyebrows, replaced it. "Right, nurses might not believe it's empty.

"Before I forget, I'm here representing the bishop with a message. He says to tell you that he was wrong about you and your wife, and a bit humbled by judging you when you obviously were struggling to follow God's will. Father Kohler has requested you be his assistant in the upcoming parish merger, and the bishop says he's happy to have you become a permanent fixture at Guardian Angels. You and Virginia are welcome to continue to live at the rectory and the diocese will cover your wages, including while you are recuperating."

"I'm honored. I'd like to stay, and I think I can say that we, Virginia and I, both appreciate his offer and support."

Father Morris grinned. "The bishop may have been wrong about you but I wasn't."

"How so?"

"I knew you should minister among people. Sounds to me that Virginia is exactly what you needed to believe that for yourself."

"She has certainly taught me a lot that I didn't think I needed to learn."

"Funny how marriage seems to do that, from what my friends tell me. They say it never stops making you stretch and grow. Parenthood even more so."

Joseph nodded.

"Which reminds me, I hear congratulations are in order. You hadn't told me about Virginia being pregnant. When is she due?"

"Last I talked to you, I had just found out, but between wedding plans and the new job I guess I forgot to share the news with you. We're feeling incredibly blessed that the baby has survived all that happened, and doesn't seem any worse for it. We'll be meeting him or her in October if all continues to go well."

Joseph laughed. "Maybe we should call him Morris, if it's a boy."

"Good heavens, don't do that to the poor thing. And my Christian name is no better. I don't think you need your first born to be Balthazar."

"Seriously? I never knew that. No wonder you go by Bud."

"Well, I don't encourage students to be on a first name basis with me, but from now on you may call me Father Bud."

He stood. "I try to never stay long on my first visit to someone in the hospital. I know how tiring company can be, and even if you aren't a germaphobe anymore, I know you're still an introvert, so I'll be on my way."

He assumed a serious manner, raised his hand, and made the sign of a cross. "May God bless and heal you, in the name of the Father, and of the Son, and of the Holy Spirit."

"Amen, and thank you," Joseph added. "Please come back when you have time. Sounds like I'm going to be here a while."

They shook hands once more, which brought Joseph a deep sense of satisfaction.

Chapter 14

Within two weeks, Virginia returned home to the very large, very empty rectory. She realized she had never lived alone before. When Virginia wasn't visiting Joseph, who had been moved to a rehab center for physical and occupational therapy, Claire kept her company during the day. Parishioners were always dropping by with parish business that Claire handled, but the lonely evenings stretched on and, though she hadn't told anyone, she often woke from nightmares. Then she would lie alert, listening to the small creaks and settling sounds an old home makes, trying to reassure herself that her enemies could no longer get to her.

Sunday after Mass, Virginia felt she needed to get away.

"Claire, would you like to visit Mercy Convent with me? You could drive Joseph's car."

"I would! Sounds like a perfect Sunday afternoon."

Panda now spent most of his days at the rehab center, working with Joseph and learning about the care he'd need when he came home, so they were on their own. Virginia marveled at her freedom to make her own plans, now that Shank and Blade were behind bars. She called ahead to the convent, and they were soon on their way.

"Virginia?" Claire didn't take her eyes off the road. "When you asked me if I'd ever considered marriage, had you learned about the cancer and were trying to set me up with Joseph in case you didn't make it?"

Virginia grinned. "Saw right through me, huh?"

"Not at the time, but I wondered about it once we learned about your tumor." She merged onto the highway. "That was sweet, you know. I'm honored that you thought of me, both for Joseph and your baby. But I'm also delighted that God had other plans."

"Me, too, Claire. He can do amazing things that we'd never figure out for ourselves."

"Amen! I'm trying to place my trust in him to show me my path."

"You said you've written to convents. Have you visited others?"

"I have. None ever struck the chord that made me know they were a good fit for me." She laughed. "They say it's like finding the right person to marry, you just at some point know for sure."

"Well, I can't say I knew right away when I met Joseph, but God made his plan seem like the only path possible. I think he had to do that with me, since I wasn't great at figuring things out on my own, or realizing when he was nudging me along."

"But at some point, you knew?"

"Absolutely. Though I wasn't completely convinced until after we were married. That's a little risky. I wouldn't recommend you dive in the way I did before you're certain."

"Well, maybe today will be the day."

Virginia directed her to the convent and it wasn't long before Sister Angela was meeting them at the door. Virginia hugged her, introduced Claire, and then asked, "Sister, does anyone else answer this door, or is it assigned to you?"

The quiet nun bowed her head a little. "I used to be quite shy. Then I challenged myself to make hospitality one of my acts of service. I express it by welcoming our guests when they come

170

and then providing tea. Oh, and cookies. I always keep a stash of cookies ready, though I must admit, that's partly because I love sweets myself."

She escorted them to the small parlor where Mother Margaret arrived with another embrace for Virginia. "Oh, my dear, we've been praying for your healing. Wonderful to see you up and about. You look a bit pale, but otherwise quite fit!"

"I'm much better, thank you. And I certainly appreciate your prayers. Please keep praying for Joseph. He struggles but is determined to adjust. He doesn't give in to self-pity, like I suspect I would." Her familiar pang of guilt for being part of the reason Joseph couldn't walk accompanied the words. Best to change the subject.

"Mother, this is Claire Davis, whom I mentioned on the phone. She's been a Godsend to the parish and me particularly."

The nun took Claire's hand. "You are very welcome, Claire. I hope you might find what you are looking for with us. The right match among the women in a convent makes service much easier. We won't take it personally, of course, if another setting works better for you, but if this is God's will for you, we'd be delighted." She turned to Virginia. "The friends you sent are leaving us one-by-one, but those who remain are in the larger parlor. Why don't you visit them while Claire and I tour the building and grounds?"

The women were happy to see Virginia again, and she chatted with them, asking where the others had gone and learning what direction the remaining ones pursued. Several nuns were relaxing in the parlor as well, reading, crocheting, and writing letters. A gentle calm permeated the room, a feminine strength that put Virginia at ease.

Sister Angela entered with her tray of tea and the promised cookies. A heavy-set, older nun slammed her book closed and hurried out of the room, grumbling, "You are no help at all, Sister Angela."

Shocked, Virginia's image of paradise crumbled a bit.

Sister Angela looked sheepish but grinned. "Sister Bernadette is on a diet. She loves cookies as much as I do." She didn't seem disturbed by the outburst and quickly passed the tray, handing out napkins and cookies as she went.

An hour passed before Claire returned wearing a dreamy look. She visited with a few of the sisters in the parlor, then she and Virginia prepared to leave.

Mother Margaret stopped them near the door. "Virginia, I want to thank you for suggesting the displaced women come to us. We've experienced a new, vibrant spirit in our home. I want you to know, I've met with certain officials, and we will become a resource for state-wide police departments. Your ladies will be the first of many, God willing."

Virginia didn't know how to show her delight, so she let a hug speak for her. God willing! What a miracle it would be for human trafficking to be overcome. All things are possible with God, she remembered. Especially when people hear him and follow.

On the drive home, Claire told Virginia all about her tour, the visit with Mother Margaret, and interviewing with the sister who worked with novices. Virginia thought Claire looked and sounded like a young woman newly in love.

She wouldn't be surprised if Claire would be leaving them soon, but she certainly would miss her. The rectory needed more people, not fewer.

Virginia needed her husband.

Joseph was sweating with exertion. To be released, his arms would have to be strong enough to hoist himself in and out of his chair using a suspended bar. Thank heavens for Griz. Panda, he corrected himself. Virginia was right. The name suited him. Panda helped him with another set of exercise repetitions.

"I've been doing a lot of thinking about my decision to be a pacifist," his friend said.

"How so?" Joseph really didn't have the breath to say more.

"I swore off shooting at the end of my service. I told you about that, right?"

"You did."

"But I keep wondering what I'd have done if I'd been there to stop Blade when he was ready to fire on you and Miz

Virginia."

Joseph stopped mid-repetition.

"I mean, what if I'd had my rifle and him in my crosshairs. Would I have fired? I keep wondering if I would. Am I wrong to say I'm a pacifist? Blade certainly was an evil that needed to be stopped."

"Panda, I'm glad you weren't given that choice. And I understand. I wonder myself about how I, someone who professes love and forgiveness, took such satisfaction in breaking the man's arm. Maybe God was good not to have it be a handgun I kicked from his hand."

"A big part of me wishes I'd been there to stop him before he made it back to the car and the gun."

Joseph shook his head sadly. "You know, it turned out being my dad's sidearm that Blade used. He stole it from my house. Maybe if we hadn't kept it as a sentimental reminder of my dad..."

Panda shrugged. "I guess maybes and what-ifs don't do any good, do they?"

"No. I'd say God worked things out better than if it had all been up to me or you. I'm not saying God made him fire those bullets, but the good Lord took Blade's evil and turned it into good by making that bullet nestle right next to Virginia's cancer.

"Here's another thought," Joseph continued, "Father Mike says he's talking to Blade. It took him a few tries before Blade got bored enough or ready enough to listen, but if anyone can save that man's soul, it's Father Mike. That couldn't have happened if we had taken his life."

Joseph started his weight lifting again, but both men were lost in thought.

At last Virginia was given a date, one week away, when Joseph would be released into her willing care and Panda's capable, well-trained hands. Their burly friend stood with her now, at the bottom of the long rectory staircase, looking up.

"No way he's going to be able to sleep up there anymore, Miz Virginia," he said slowly.

"You're right, of course. I hadn't thought about that. Time

for some serious rearranging. He'll need—I guess, *we* will need—a bedroom down here." She felt herself blush a little. They hadn't really shared a bed before, but things were different now. How different, she wasn't sure.

"Sounds like the old priest won't be coming back, and Father Kohler says that he'll keep living at the other parish. I'd guess that means you get to decide where you want to put what."

Virginia grinned at the logical man. He was right! Suddenly the rectory felt like it truly was her home. She wandered through the main floor and chose a large, bright room currently holding several circular tables and chairs. "Panda, if you'll help me, I think we can dedicate this meeting room to another purpose." She imagined her little twin bed snuggled next to Joseph's. She was pretty sure neither of them wanted to sleep apart anymore.

She had been trying to talk to God like a friend lately. She sent up a quick prayer. *Grandma's God*—she still liked that title, though he was certainly becoming her own God now—*please show Joseph that physical love can be holy when a couple is married. And help me to realized that making love can be worlds away from what I was forced to do. Let me feel it as holy, too.*

Then a new idea struck her. "Panda, let's go shopping!"

Chapter 15

Ten days later, the congregation applauded as Father Mike invited Joseph up to the microphone. He wheeled himself up the aisle and, using the new ramp the parishioners had built, onto the altar platform. He turned to his parish.

"I want to thank you all for your prayers. Believe me, I could feel them. I also want to say, 'Good thing Father Mike has taken over as pastor, or you might not have ever gotten another priest. Between heart attacks and bullets, word is out that this is one dangerous assignment!'" He laughed, and the congregation joined him.

The parish had been told about the merger with Blessed Trinity. Though the bishop expected a strong reaction, most people seemed to accept the decision with relief. Blending the parishes would mean shared finances, and that prospect calmed the different factions at Guardian Angels.

Joseph looked out among the parishioners as he rolled back down the ramp. He passed his pew to shake hands along the whole aisle. There was Sam Jorgen sitting next to Susan Burke. Well, that was an interesting development. Dr. Knightly, the principal, was seated with some of the other school staff, who all seemed less stressed than the last time he'd seen them. In fact, all the congregation faces were more relaxed than any time he'd stood before them. One whole row of his veteran friends, including Panda, stood and took turns grinning and shaking hands with him. They had finished the painting of both the rectory and the church, inside and out. Now that summer vacation had begun, they planned to spend their Saturdays on the school.

But the very happiest face waited for him to return to their front pew, which had been shortened so his chair would fit. His beautiful wife glowed with second-trimester joy. She had recovered quickly from her surgery, and he prayed she would overcome all the trauma she'd experienced. Joseph had suggested she attend counseling while he and Panda struggled through his regular physical therapy. Virginia's counselor had encouraged her to buy a good camera, and she had spent a whole afternoon showing him her photos his second day home.

They both worked hard to heal, and his body and her spirit were strengthening steadily, though they each found themselves tiring easily, both of them from the damage their bodies had suffered, and her from the incredible feat of growing a child inside her.

One of his favorite parts of each day was only a few hours away. He didn't know how long their recovery and the coming baby would work as an excuse, but each afternoon when lunch was cleared away, Claire would take over the front desk, and they would relish siesta time. Together they'd settle into their new queen-sized bed that filled what had once been the first-floor meeting room. They simply nestle together until they both were asleep. They would take it slowly. They had all their lives ahead of them, and they planned to treasure every moment.

Epilogue

Panda Sullivan waited outside the police station until Joseph rolled into sight. Then he jumped out of the van to help his friend get seated and stow the wheelchair.

"How'd your day go?" he asked, like he did each time he drove Joseph home after his chaplain work.

"It was a hard day, but good. An officer was injured, but thank God, not critically. I met with his family at the hospital and did what I could to help them until the surgeon brought the good news."

"You're a blessing to the police force. Between them and us vets, you're probably one of the best loved chaplains around." He started the van and pulled out carefully. "I don't know how you find time for it all and still handle the parish work, too."

"You make it possible! You're a blessing to me and my family, Panda. You take up the slack and keep us all coping. Thriving even! You sure we aren't too big a burden?"

"Burden!?! You're family! It all works out fine. When you don't need me, I get my maintenance work done for Father Mike at the parishes. It's all good."

"Have Mom and Meg arrived?"

"I picked them up at the airport and they're waiting at the

rectory. Fr. Mike is on his way there, too."

They chatted more as they drove, and Joseph thanked God like he'd done many times before for bringing this gentle bear into their lives.

When they arrived, Panda lifted him out of the van and into his chair. Joseph wheeled himself up the ramp to the rectory front door and they entered. The aromas that met him were heavenly. He rolled toward the kitchen.

Fr. Mike, Fr. Bud, and Meg were already seated at the dining table, and he experienced the strangest sense of déjà vu. Sitting in her highchair, their sweet one-year-old Hannah Ruth mashed a cupcake into her mouth. Her eyes widened with the delight of her first taste of frosting.

His mother carried a bowl of steaming spaghetti to the table and laughed. "She couldn't wait until dessert for her birthday cupcake?"

"Her arms are longer than I thought. She reached right over and grabbed the cupcake," Meg said. "I wasn't going to be the mean auntie and take it away."

His mom and sister greeted Joseph with hugs. He shook the men's hands and welcomed them.

Virginia set down a bowl of her delicious meat sauce on the table. "Come on, Panda, pull up to the table. We don't want the pasta to get cold." She greeted Joseph with a kiss, and he rested his hand near her rising waistline.

"I felt this little man move for the first time today," she whispered to him. "Soon, you'll be able to, too."

Their second child was on the way, and he worried about how he could possibly love another little one as much as he loved Hannah. Of course, they weren't sure yet that it was a boy, and in truth it didn't matter to him whether it was a boy or girl. The idea that the love he and Virginia shared created a new life was enough for him to nearly burst with joy.

"Joseph, I hear your parish work is going well," his mother said after they finished the blessing.

"Surprisingly well. The months we spent to make the transition as smooth as possible, meeting with parishioners at both locations and listening to their concerns, has paid off. We've survived our first month of full school integration without much fallout. Grades one through four meet here on our campus. Grades five through eight at the other campus, with both hosting a kindergarten. That had been the final sticking point. Parents didn't want their littlest ones going to a strange new place for their first year of schooling."

"So far, so good," Father Mike interjected as he broke off a piece of Virginia's bread and passed the loaf along.

Joseph continued, "We've blended the finances between the two old parishes, which has reduced my worries considerably. People still call the church buildings Blessed Trinity and Guardian Angels, but we renamed the combined parish Holy Family, to reflect our commitment to behave like one big clan."

"Sounds like you and Father Mike have figured out dividing the responsibilities," his mother said as she pushed the pasta bowl within his reach.

"Father Mike's the boss, and I'm happy with that." Joseph served himself a large helping of spaghetti.

"You can't believe how much Joseph does to ease the burden. He handles most administration details, which leaves me more free time to spend with our parishioners."

"And Fr. Mike's fine with me being on call for chaplaincy to the police station and the area's vets." He nodded his appreciation at his friend. "I feel like I get the best of both worlds and am working from my strengths rather than struggling against my weaknesses."

"Well, you've certainly overcome a lot in the past year, you and Virginia." She rested her hand momentarily on her daughter-in-law's shoulder.

"I had a letter from Claire," Virginia announced. "She's loving life in the novitiate. She says Mother Margaret sends her regards to all. Oh, and though they now have a third set of girls to keep them busy, the last of my ladies left them this week. Edith has finished dental assistant school, been hired, and moved to her own apartment."

Fr. Bud shook his head in amazement. "I never would have dreamed what lay ahead on the day Joseph brought you into my office and introduced you, Virginia. You two have made such a difference in so many lives. Mother Margaret tells me she and Virginia have been visiting other convents to encourage them to become safe havens, as well."

Joseph watched the color come to Virginia's cheeks and thanked God again that his beautiful wife came into his life.

"Where do the women tend to end up when they leave the convent?" Meg asked.

"Several have found work as waitresses or in offices." Virginia answered. "The parishioners here have been very generous with their help, training and hiring them." She cut and blew on some spaghetti noodles and set them on Hannah's tray. "One entered the novitiate with Claire. Some were reunited early on with their families."

"Well, even though I'll be heading to college next year, I think being with family is the very best place in the world," Meg said, and they all nodded.

"Amen." Panda punctuated the word with his bright smile, for he truly was considered family now.

What a blessing, Joseph thought, to have their loved ones together to celebrate their daughter's first birthday.

Virginia wiped Hannah's face and hands, lifted her out of her highchair, and set her on her daddy's lap. He nuzzled the baby's face and Hannah giggled before nestling against his chest. Joseph called to mind one of his favorite translations of Hosea 11:4. *God said, "I drew them to me with affection and love. I picked them up and held them to my cheek."*

He had always respected God the Father, but now he related to Abba, the Papa God, who held his loved ones up to snuggle against his cheek.

For a brief instant, his mind glimpsed a rainbow-filled place, and a sense of incredible joy and peace washed over him.

The End

ABOUT THE AUTHOR

Betty Arrigotti mixes faith, friendship, and family in her life and in her stories. She has been married 40 years, raised daughters worthy of praise, and believes that her grandchildren are blessings from above. She treasures her friends and delights in the world of nature. An introvert like her hero, she strives to balance her need for time alone and the world's need for what she can offer. You can get to know her better and learn about her other novels at www.BettyArrigotti.com. Email her at Betty@Arrigotti.com.

Made in the USA
San Bernardino, CA
10 October 2017